GYAEHLINGAAY

GYAEHLINGAAY

Traditions, Tales, and Images of the Kaigani Haida

by

Carol M. Eastman and Elizabeth A. Edwards

traditional stories told by

Lillian Pettviel and other Haida elders

illustrated by

Duane Pasco

Published by Burke Museum Publications, Seattle

Distributed by the University of Washington Press
Seattle and London

Thomas Burke Memorial Washington State Museum Monograph 6

Museum Monographs
1. Bill Holm. 1965. *Northwest Coast Indian Art: An Analysis of Form.*
2. Bill Holm and George Quimby. 1980. *Edward S. Curtis in the Land of the War Canoes: A Pioneer Cinematographer in the Pacific Northwest.*
3. Bill Holm. 1983. *Smoky-Top: The Art and Times of Willie Seaweed.*
4. Bill Holm. 1987. *Spirit and Ancestor: A Century of Northwest Coast Indian Art at the Burke Museum.*
5. Patrick V. Kirch. 1989. *Niuatoputapu: The Prehistory of a Polynesian Chiefdom.*
6. Carol M. Eastman and Elizabeth A. Edwards. 1991. *gyaehlingaay: Traditions, Tales, and Images of the Kaigani Haida.* Stories as told by Lillian Pettviel and other Haida elders. Illustrated by Duane Pasco.
7. *A Time of Gathering: Native Heritage in Washington State.* 1991. Edited by Robin K. Wright.

Copyright ©1991 by the Thomas Burke Memorial Washington State Museum.
Printed in the United States of America.
Cover designed by Audrey Meyer.

Burke Museum Publications Program
Dr. Sievert Rohwer, Director
Dr. Susan Libonati-Barnes, Editor
Lori Starrs, Copyeditor
Jenifer Young, Editorial Associate
Christine Kleinke, Editorial Assistant

Library of Congress Cataloging-in-Publication Data
Eastman, Carol M.
    Gyaehlingaay: traditions, tales, and images of the Kaigani Haida
by Carol M. Eastman and Elizabeth A. Edwards; traditional stories told by
Lillian Pettviel and other Haida elders; illustrated by Duane Pasco.

    p. cm. – (The Thomas Burke Memorial Washington State Museum
monograph; 6)

    Includes bibliographical references.

    ISBN 0-295-96824-9

    1. Haida Indians–Legends. 2. Haida language–Texts, I. Edwards,
Elizabeth A., 1939- . II. Pettviel, Lillian. III. Pasco, Duane. IV. Title. V.
Series: Monograph (Thomas Burke Memorial Washington State Museum); 6.

E99.H2E27 1991   89.1733
398.2'089972–dc20   CIP

Contents

List of Figures

Introduction

gyáehling is the Kaigani Haida word for "story." To *gyaehlandáa* is to tell a story for a purpose, that is, to amuse, to transmit cultural information, or to impart a moral lesson. *Gyáehlingaay* are stories told on a winter evening in precontact Alaska as well as around the kitchen table in Seattle today.

The Alaskan dialect of Haida, called Kaigani, is a composite of at least three northern dialects of the language from the villages of Kasaan, Howkan, and Klinkwan on Prince of Wales Island in Southeast Alaska. Prince of Wales and the surrounding Alaskan islands are north of the Queen Charlottes, where Canadian speakers of the Masset dialect live (see map 1, p. 2). A third language center exists on the southern part of the Queen Charlotte Islands and includes Skidegate and the now-extinct Ninstints dialect.

We have provided each grouping of stories with an ethnohistorical introduction and a brief discussion of form and content. An English translation of each story is followed, in a section that begins on page 45, by a line-by-line presentation that alternates Haida, a literal English translation, and then a free translation. This approach is intended to highlight differences between what is said and meant in Haida and the text's approximation in English, to provide as much meaning as possible for both speakers of English and the Kaigani people, who we hope will read and enjoy the stories.

Since the early 1970s we have been studying various aspects of the Kaigani dialect of Haida and have published a number of papers describing and analyzing certain linguistic structures of the language. Since 1975, this work has been done in conjunction with Lillian Pettviel, who either has served as the primary language consultant for our research or has been instrumental in providing access to other native-speaking Haida people. Mistakes and inconsistencies in transcription and analysis are entirely the fault of the authors and do not reflect the truly insightful approach of Pettviel to the study of her native tongue. The narrative selections in this volume are byproducts of our linguistic research and a natural outcome of our close friendship. Throughout this book we will be referring to our work and that of other linguists in footnotes. We will point out in nontechnical language some of the striking characteristics of the sounds and structure of this beautiful language.

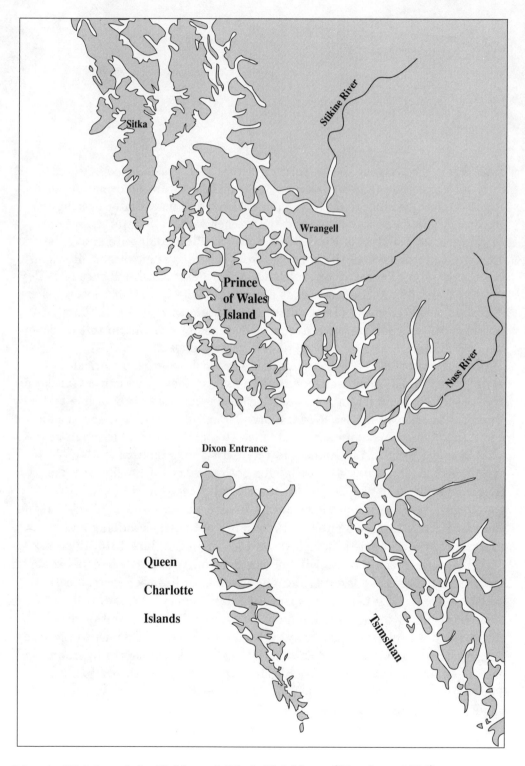

Map 1: Vicinity of the Haida and Their Neighbors (Vaughan, 1984)

The first narrative, that of the Haida migration to Southeast Alaska, was told by Pettviel's father, Jim Edenso, to Dr. J. Daniel Vaughan when the latter was conducting his doctoral research in Alaska between 1977 and 1980. The story was related to us in Haida in 1984 by Pettviel. During discussions of this story we showed her an English translation of a Skidegate story that had been published by the Bureau of Indian Affairs in 1911 and asked if she would attempt a retelling in the Kaigani dialect so we could see how the dialects compared. This story in Kaigani Haida became the second narrative of this book.

The stories we present as reminiscences were told spontaneously while we were listening to, and attempting to participate in, conversations among several Haida speakers who on various occasions included Pettviel, Louise Arrington, Margaret Cogo, Winnie Bartlett, and Annabel and David Peel. The psalm was given to us as an Easter gift in 1984 after a discussion of how devout Haida pray in their language. We asked for the recipe for fried bread off the record and include it here because of its obvious narrative structure. "The Octopus Story" and "Raven Finds Water" were retold by Pettviel and two Haida guests in her home and are based on a small booklet of Haida stories told by Robert Cogo (Cogo 1979). "The Story of *qaao qaao*" was told in English by David Peel at a laboratory session at the University of Washington in the spring of 1983 and later retold in Haida by Pettviel.

Lillian Pettviel was born in Hydaburg, Alaska, the daughter of Jim and Linda Edenso. She attended a government school for native children, where the use of the Haida language was strictly forbidden. Later she went to Sheldon Jackson School (now Sheldon Jackson Community College) in Sitka. As an adult she has resided in various parts of the "lower 48," practicing the Haida language by herself to stave off homesickness. When she lived in Seattle and San Francisco she often conversed with other Haida speakers. Like many expatriate Alaskan natives, Lillian made regular trips home to Alaska during which she indulged her desire to retain the language in long talks with her father and others of his generation. Southeast Alaskan Haida people, for the most part, have strong connections to the Seattle area, the nearest mainland U.S. city. As American rather than Canadian Indians, they exist in a kind of cultural diaspora despite ritual and personal ties to the Masset Haida people of the Queen Charlottes. Pettviel and a number of her Kaigani-speaking friends meet in Seattle from time to time just to speak Haida; she and her friends were kind enough to tape record some of their sessions for our use in the "reminiscences" and "tales" sections of this book.

Images evoked by these Haida stories have been illustrated by Northwest Coast artist Duane Pasco, using both traditional and modern Northwest Coast art forms. Pasco was born in the Puget Sound area but spent much of his childhood in Alaska. A carpenter and structural iron worker by trade, he has been an artist all his life. He began carving and painting traditional Northwest Coast Indian art in about 1968. Bill Holm's analysis of nineteenth-century Pacific Northwest Coast art, says Pasco, made it possible for him and other twentieth-century carvers and seriographers to work with skill and confidence in this difficult art form (Holm 1965). Pasco is now a lecturer on principles of design in Northwest Coast Indian art and has displayed his work at numerous art galleries in the Pacific Northwest. He has been commissioned to produce a large number of objects for commercial and public display as well as works for native ritual use.

With the exception of the illustrations, this manuscript was prepared using (LaTeX), a special version of the (TeX) formatting program invented by Donald Knuth of Stanford University. We wish to acknowledge the many hours of technical advice provided by Stacy Waters of the Humanities and Arts Computing Center at the University of Washington. We also wish to thank Steve Graham of Arts and Sciences Computing at the University of Washington for his support of this project.

How to Read Haida

Some letters may be read and pronounced the same in Haida as in English (e.g., b, ch, d, g, h, j, k, l, m, n, p, s, t, w, y). Haida uses other English letters differently to represent sounds present in Haida but not in English. Letters used to represent vowels in Haida represent sounds specific to that language.[1]

Haida a	sounds like English	u	in	'but'
Haida aa	sounds like English	a	in	'father'
Haida ae	sounds like English	a	in	'bat'
Haida i	sounds like English	i	in	'pin'
Haida ii	sounds like English	i	in	'machine'
Haida u	sounds like English	u	in	'put'
Haida uu	sounds like English	oo	in	'moon'
Haida o	sounds like English	oa	in	'boat'
Haida ei	sounds like English	ei	in	'neighbor'
Haida aay	sounds like English	y	in	'my'
Haida aao	sounds like English	ow	in	'cow'

Stress marks indicate which syllable of a word is stressed.[2] Some letters that never occur at the beginning of a word in English may begin a Haida word. For example, Haida words may begin with or contain:

ng	in English	'sing'
dl	in English	'ladle'

---

[1] See also Leer 1977:12-18. We have tried throughout this book to adhere to the orthographic system developed by the Haida themselves, in a workshop sponsored by the Alaska Native Language Center in Ketchikan in the 1970s, with the following exceptions: we do not mark preglottalization of consonants (though we may occasionally insert an epenthetic vowel), we do not put glottal stops before word initial vowels, we use G for g and q for k̲, and we mark intonation instead of high and low tone.

[2] Division of the spoken narrative into word-length units is entirely arbitrary, though we drew on examples of printed Haida and other linguistic works where possible. Often we relied on sentence intonation to determine word boundaries. See Enrico (1980) for the best current explanation of stress assignment in the language.

tl   in English   'footlight'[3]
ts   as in English   'cats'

What is pronounced 'ts' in a Haida word becomes 'ch' when a Haida person uses that word in an English context.[4] To read Haida, one also needs to know about some special letters that represent sounds not present in English:

G   pronounced with a raspy throat, sort of a cough
hl   pronounced the way the Welsh say Ll in Llewelyn
q   pronounced like k but farther back in the throat
k'   k accompanied by glottal closure, a rapid ejection of air to make a popping soun
q'   same as k' but farther back in the throat
x   pronounced like <u>ch</u> in German 'ich' [5]
X   pronounced like <u>ch</u> in german 'ach' [6]

We hope these symbols will enable a Haida speaker who reads English but does not read or write Haida to read aloud the narratives in this collection. Given dialectical differences, the fact of rapid language change, and personal variation, some Haida speakers may not agree with the way words have been written here; yet, we hope we have been able to represent spoken Haida in a way that is intelligible and pleasing to the native ear. For specialists interested in a more detailed analysis of the Haida phonological system, symbols to represent further distinctions in the language are needed. Various systems for describing the sounds of Haida may be found in Leer 1977, Eastman and Aoki 1978, and Enrico 1980.

---

[3] Actually, the 't' of 'tl' is a sound made farther back in the throat than the ordinary 't.' We practiced the 'tl' sound by repeating the phrase 'tleen the tlams in the closet' with our minds set on the 'k' sound of 'clean the clams in the closet' but our tongues in place for 'tl.'

[4] For example, in a Haida story about the settlement of Alaska, the Raven calls out *"ts'aats, ts'aats"* at a place called Ts'aats Ts'uunii, which appears on maps today as Chaats Chuunii or Čačini.

[5] A voiceless fricative at the soft palate but pronounced a little farther forward than <u>x</u>.

[6] A voiceless fricative at the soft palate but pronounced a little farther back than <u>x</u>.

The Stories

Eleven different Kaigani Haida stories are presented in these pages. The very act of putting titles on verbal art forms indicates an essential difference between the Haida "performances" and the English "literary events" we are juxtaposing. The stories range from short reminiscences to longer historical narratives and animal tales, and illustrate the way Haida narrative structure incorporates Western oral genres. Illustrations are intended to evoke aspects of content, context, and mood.

Some grammatical structures of Haida lend a particular flair to their English translation. We hope that what seems to be unusual English grammar and awkward, redundant phrasing in the translations will lead readers to see things from a Haida point of view. We feel that literal translations of certain constructions represent the prose more faithfully. For example, where an English speaker would say "I tell a story" or "I pick berries," a speaker of Haida would say "I story-tell" or "I story-make," and "I berry-pick." Verbs come at the end of Haida sentences, and the point the sentence makes is mentioned at the beginning.[7] "Fish-is-what-I-eat" is a typical example of constituent order in Haida, as is "The-bear-is-what-the-man-killed." Keeping the English translation close to the Haida and including such nuances, even at the expense of the English, allows a sense of the Haida way with words to come through.

Early in "The Story of *qaao qaao*" we read that "one person understands raven language." The statement introduces a person (topic) and comments on a quality of that person. It is this person whose actions will become the subject of further information that is important in moving the story line along. Subsequent sentences in the narrative start with reference to this utterance as "the one who understands raven language," which is later shortened to "the raven language understander." This topic-comment format of Haida utterances forces the tale-teller into a redundancy of style that adds wonderfully to the audience's feeling of participation. Individual utterances are affected by this format as well. In "The Migration from Masset," we hear, "and then at the

---

[7]This point has been described as the "new information," the "topic," and the "focus" of the sentence. See Edwards 1982, 1983; Halliday 1967.

place where they lived too, *chaats chuunii* is what they called it," and "the weather was so bad and cold but that's the reason I told you about when Raven saved them," and finally, "anyplace when they first found water was running, now that place is theirs; we say Hedda Creek."[8] In English we might just as easily start the first sentence with "*chaats chuunii*," the second with "the reason I told you," and the third with "Hedda Creek."

Other examples of the Haida way of speaking are seen in other texts. For example, in "Raven Finds Water" when the Island Spirit forgot he had lied to Raven he says, "That there was no water to be found is what he said" instead of "He told Raven there was no water to be found." One sentence in "The Octopus Story," translates literally into English as "what-thing-children-did, people-to-he-told," though in a free translation it comes out "He told the people what the children had done."

In Haida narrative there is a tendency to say things twice. This is especially noticeable in the story "Raven Finds Water." For example, when Raven visits the Island Spirit, a battle of wits ensues. Raven has no intention of leaving before the Island Spirit gives him some clue as to where the water is. The teller sings, "waited for him, waited for him" to convey a sense of time passing with little being accomplished. Later, Raven says to Island Spirit, "You stink really bad, you stink really bad," and, "Do bathe yourself, do bathe yourself," in an attempt to get Island Spirit to reveal the location of the water hole by getting water for a bath. Other sentence pairs exist in "The Octopus Story": "He told the people what the children had done" and "he told the people the result of what the children had done." In "The Story of *qaao qaao*," the ravens chant, "here is the Chief, here is the Chief."

Another storytelling convention is to use the present tense at exciting points in the story. In "The Migration from Masset," when neighbors begin to get curious about the activities of the *q'wiitaas xaatáay*, "the muddy-mouth people," the narrator has them say, "What are the *q'wii xaatáas* people up to? Why are they making so many boats? What are they up to?" The same device is used in "Raven Finds Water" and "The Story of *qaao qaao*."

Episodes in oral narrative are divided by the use of conjunctions such as "and," "and then," "after that," and "meanwhile."[9] To an English-speaking reader the language may seem repetitive, but to a Haida-speaking listener the conjunctions indicate that a new character is about to be introduced or the action is to take a new turn. The clearest examples of this occur in the final sections of many narratives where *waadluu* ("and then") clearly indicates that

---

[8] Hedda Creek is variously referred to as Hetta Creek, Hetta Inlet, or Hedda Inlet.
[9] See Eastman and Edwards 1984; Hymes 1981.

a turn of events is about to happen and *asgaayst* ("after that") seems to designate the concluding piece of action. In "The Story of *qaao qaao*" such conjunctions act as contextualizing cues to break the story into memorable chunks and to help the audience follow the story line.[10]

We begin with a narrative describing the origin of the Kaigani people. "The Migration from Masset" is the Kaigani view of how they came to be on Prince of Wales Island. Map 2 (p. 10) shows both Haida locales, i.e., Masset and Prince of Wales Island. Next we present a Kaigani rendering of a story found in a 1911 Haida grammar by John Swanton. The story tells of a raid made by Skidegate Haida on their Bella Coola neighbors. Both of these narratives reveal a view of Northwest Coast history which stands in contrast to the more usual accounts given by missionaries, explorers, and early ethnographers.

Reminiscences follow, of growing up as a Kaigani Haida in the early decades of this century. "The First Kill," "Mother's Brother's First Kill," and "Paul's Name"[11] tell of ceremonially important events while "The Scaredest I Have Ever Been in My Life" gives a sense of day-to-day living in a family that relied on fish for cash income. The Kaigani Psalm and recipe show the adaptation of English prose to Haida.

Three Haida animal tales complete the eleven narrative pieces we present as Haida *gyáehlingaay*. These reveal important aspects of the way the world is, and is supposed to be, according to Haida beliefs.

---

[10] See Gumperz 1979, 1984; Eastman and Edwards 1984.
[11] We are indebted to Louise Arrington for this charming story.

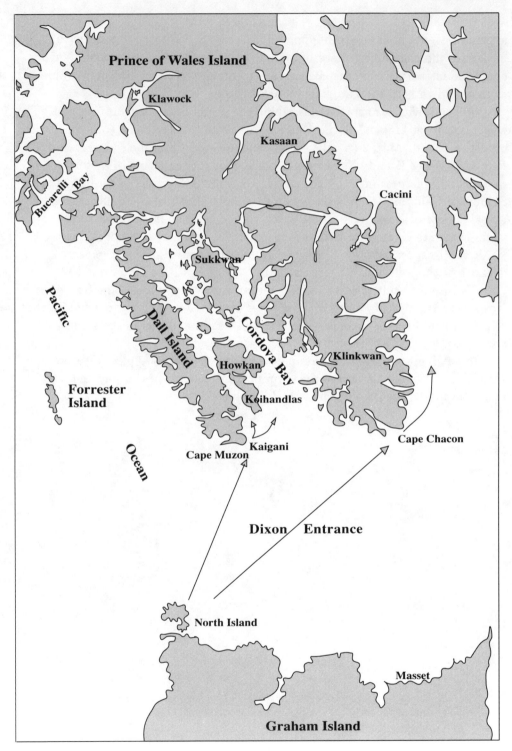

Map 2: The Alaskan Migration Routes (Vaughan, 1984)

Traditions

As early as the first decade of this century, John Swanton (1911) recorded that the ancestral home of the Haida language was the Queen Charlotte Islands off the coast of British Columbia. The language had been called Skiitagetan in an early classification of North American Indian languages (Powell 1880). In addition to the Skidegate, Masset, and Kaigani divisions of the language, Swanton mentioned another, a southern dialect, called Ninstints after the principal town of its speakers. The Ninstints people were referred to in Swanton's story as coming to the Skidegate people at Kaisun for aid in carrying out a raid on the Bella Coola people who lived across the water on the coast of British Columbia. We have no data on the Haida dialect that might have been spoken at Ninstints, south of Skidegate. However, it is thought that a southernmost dialect of Haida did exist and was spoken there.

"About a hundred and fifty or two hundred years ago, ... a large body of Haida moved from their old towns in the northwestern part of the islands and settled around Cordova and Kasaan Bays, Alaska" (Swanton 1911:209). As we can see in the following ethnohistorical account, this move was accomplished in at least two waves: first the *q'wiitaas xaatáay* ("the muddy-mouth people") landed at Cape Chacon and moved up the southeast coast of the island; later, the *yáadaas* ("honorable people") left Graham Island and came ashore at Cape Muzon. The language of these two groups of Haida, who were from the vicinity of Masset, evolved into distinct but closely related dialects spoken in Howkan, Klinkwan, and Kasaan and known collectively as Kaigani Haida. Map 3 of Prince of Wales Island (p. 28) shows these Kaigani Haida villages.

Several authorities agree with Swanton's version of the Kaigani migration, which took place shortly after the Indians' first contact with Europeans (Vaughan 1984:2; Dawson 1881:104; Murdoch 1934:222; Gunther 1972:124; Blackman 1973:7). In the north, the Alaskan Tlingit were the nearest neighbors of the Masset people and served as a lure to the people now known as Kaigani to move there. The view that migrating Haida displaced Tlingit groups is evidenced by retained Tlingit place names for the new Haida town sites on Prince of Wales Island (Vaughan 1984:3). Our story of the migration is really the story of two groups, as remembered by Pettviel from stories she heard as a child. The migrant Haida occupied villages on both sides of Prince of Wales Island and called themselves *Gaats xaadáay*, or "people of the strait" (see Hodge 1905:522), though in the oral history of the area they consist of two groups, *q'wii xaatáas* and *yáadaas*. The name Kaigani refers to these Alaskan Haida collectively and was the Tlingit name of a village site at Cape Muzon on the southern tip of Dall Island (see map 2).

This narrative account of how the Haida moved to Alaska accords well
with the archival record. The *q'wiitaas xaatáay* probably moved during the
late seventeenth and early eighteenth century (Dawson 1880:104; Gunther
1922:119). It is likely that the *yáadaas* followed some twenty years later.
Vaughan (1984:23) provides the following account of the migration as told to
him by Pettviel's father, Jim Edenso, an elderly Haida member of the Eagle
clan. It provides a fitting context for the migration story presented here:

> Many Haida were living around Graham Island and at that place
> called Langara Island. There were many people and there was a
> shortage of food. Trouble broke out among them, but I don't know
> what caused it. The first ones to leave were the Quetas.[12] They
> could see the land across there and they decided to try and make
> their new home there. At the right time of the year they made
> themselves ready. They built large rafts and put everything they
> had on those. When the weather was right they started across.
> They landed at Cape Muzon (the southern tip of Dall Island, and
> nearest point across Dixon Entrance). They needed to find food
> (salmon) so many men were sent out to look. Then they found
> Hetta and Eek (sockeye salmon streams in Hetta Inlet). The
> Quetas people prospered their first year here and word of it got
> back to Graham Island.
>
> The next that came across were the Yadas people.[13] They started
> across too late in the season (late summer) and while coming over
> they got caught in bad weather. They couldn't see across to the
> other side where they wanted to go. They made it across but they
> missed Cape Muzon. They landed just south of Cape Chacon (the
> southern tip of Prince of Wales Island). They decided not to stay
> there and so they moved on up along the east side of Prince of
> Wales Island in search of food and a better place to stay. Winter
> was coming on and they didn't have enough food to get them
> through.
>
> They were camped over there by Chomley (Cholmendeley Inlet)
> and they were worried about what was going to happen to them
> because they couldn't find any salmon stream. They didn't know
> anything about this country they were in. While they were camped

---

[12] "Quetas" refers to the group Lillian Pettviel calls *q'wíitaas* or *q'wii xaatáas* in her account.
"Mud eater" and "muddy mouth" are equivalent terms for these people.

[13] "Yadas" is Vaughan's transcription of Pettviel's term *yáadaas*.

there, a raven would come and fly back and forth (in a figure eight) crying *tc'a tc'a*, and then would fly off, always in the same direction. This raven came back every day and did the same thing. Someone finally got the message and a couple of canoes were sent off to follow this raven the next time he came. They followed him to a stream in Chomley; that stream was just full of fish, dog salmon. They loaded their canoes with the salmon, using spears, and hurried back to camp to tell the people about it. Everybody hurried and got ready. All the men jumped into their canoes while the women gathered firewood and prepared drying-sticks. When the men returned their canoes were filled with dog salmon. They called their camp *tc'atc'ini* (Čačini) because of the way that raven spoke to them.

For quite some time, the Haida and the Tlingit shared personal and economic interests in the same area. Conflict between the groups eventually arose. Swanton (1905:89) records that while in Čačini the Yadas people were attacked by a group of Tlingit. Some were killed. When word reached Graham Island in the Queen Charlottes, a large party of Masset Haida rose to the defense of their northern relatives. Through sheer numbers and strength, the Haida soundly defeated these Tlingit. "Survivors were pursued northward towards the Tlingit village of Sukkwan which the Haida overwhelmed in further retaliation for their loss" (Swanton 1905:89-90, quoted in Vaughan 1984:25).

The migration of Haida clan groups from Graham Island then continued. The Yadas, who belonged to the Eagle clan, were joined by some Stast'as people of the Eagle clan and Taslanas of the Raven clan. The Stast'as name refers to "great numbers and wealth"; Taslanas means "those of the sandy beach." These people settled in the abandoned Tlingit village of Kasaan. Other Haida came to settle in Howkan, on Long Island, while the original Quetas (Ravens) and some Salants (Eagles) occupied Sukkwan on Sukkwan Island. The Yakwlanas, "middle-town-people" also came across and eventually settled in the old Tlingit village of Klinkwan and in a village south of Howkan on Long Island known as Quehaandlas, or "muddy-stream-town" (Vaughan 1984:25).

Migration from Masset (When the People Came North)

The story about when the people first moved to K'asaan is a long one. In the summertime everybody would move to the cannery. The Yaadaas Haida were the first ones living there, but that isn't the beginning of the story. Before that, many years ago, the q'wiitaas xaatáay *people had been the first ones to move to Alaska. This is a true story.*

When the people used to live in Masset, the q'wiitaas xáataay there were
starving. Other Haida that lived around them didn't think very highly of the q'wii
xaatáas people.[14] There's a story behind why they are called q'wii xaatáas. They
used to live in the woods and eat roots of the things that grew around them. Because
they ate roots and bark, the area around their mouths was stained a muddy color.

The way the people lived wasn't pleasant. They couldn't see their way to get
any fish or seafood. Those that lived around them, at the point and on the cove,
wouldn't let the q'wii xaatáas go fishing. And then too, other people felt a hatred
towards the q'wii xaatáay. It was said they used to fight each other.

The q'wii xaatáay got fed up with the conditions and, seeing a point of land to
the north of them, they got ready to go there. It was a long ways away. When the
weather was nice was the only time when the land was visible. Even if they had
known it was a long way from there—no matter what—any kind of living would be
better than what they were experiencing. They thought their living conditions would
be sure to improve as they got ready to move. And so they got themselves ready.

When other people first heard the news they got all excited. Among themselves
they were thinking, "I wonder what the q'wii xaatáas people are up to. I wonder why
they're making so many boats. I wonder what they're up to." The q'wiitaas xaatáay
just had the neighbors amazed. Even though the people living around them were
worried, they didn't ask them what was going on.

Without talking, the q'wii xaatáas made themselves ready. When they were all
ready the whole clan packed to leave. Afterwards the people living there heard what
happened. How they got the story I don't know. But the q'wiitaas xaatáay left,
sailing to a point up north they could see. That's all the neighbors knew.

Quite a while after that the people living around Masset heard the news that the
q'wii xaatáas were living quite well. Food was plentiful for them. Everything was
close at hand. Their really poor living conditions they had had living up the woods
from Masset now were different. Really, they were well off; all things were right at
hand and plentiful for them.

When the news flashed back, once again some of the Masset people got ready
to leave.

But they had forgotten just what time of year the q'wii xaatáas people had
moved. But they got everyone ready anyway.

They got boats ready one after the other. They got their food ready too. They
knew it was going to be a long trip so they prepared quite a bit of food.

---

[14] q'wii xaatáas and q'wii xaatáay are reduced forms of q'wiitaas xaatáay and we have left
them as they occurred in the original narrative. There is nothing sloppy about this type of
contraction; as long as the phrase has at least one s or one y it is perfectly grammatical Haida.

At last they were ready and they started sailing away. But they had a hard time. The wind was blowing severely. The weather, too, was not good. In fact, it was really bad. Once in a while the wind gave them a hard time. After they sailed a long time they came near land and rowed to it. They didn't know where they were. They landed here at Cape Chacon, down on the sand. They weren't at Kaigani. When the Spanish arrived there the Haidas started calling it Cape Chacon. Now they pronounce it exactly as they learned it from the Spanish.

They started living up north of Cape Chacon but the weather was really bad. The wind there was very stormy. It was like living at Masset, like living on the ocean side. When the weather was too tough for them some of them went out looking so they could move to another place.

For a long while they looked, moving several times.[15] When they got back the wind was so hard it made them run for safety. They landed up the creek. They didn't like it much but even then it was too stormy. It got cold with rain. They were getting desperate. So then they started building their house. They worked on the trees. They started clearing the trees and the land too.

While they were hurrying to make their homes, Raven used to fly around above them. Once in a while in the mornings he'd come there and he'd fly around above them. When he flew around above them he'd call out tsáats tsáats tsáats. *That's the only thing he'd say. After he flew around above them repeatedly for some time he'd fly away and then he'd return. Once in a while when it was getting evening he'd fly down once again. He'd always come from the same way. Then he'd fly down again the same way. And always when he flew around above them he used to say,* Tsáats, tsáats, tsáats,—tsáats.

They finally realized what he was doing, flying back down the same way. For this reason they started to be curious about him. Some men went running after him. When they got up towards the cove they arrived at a creek. Really, they were just astonished! There were a lot of fish in the creek. It was so full with dog salmon they were really excited. They threw some into the canoe any old way. Some of the men threw them onto the beach too, because they were happy, they were excited.

They rowed back fast and they called to the ones at the camp. After that, those that were left behind in the house really worked fast. They prepared the smoke house too.

"Hurry, hurry!" they called to each other. "Finish your smoke house as you go along!"

There were many fish. As was said, they all, the women too, were working hard. In the meantime the men started transporting the fish. There were really so many dog salmon, they were working on them just as fast as they could go. They were

---

[15] One of these places was Kasaan at Carta Bay.

"The wind was blowing severely. The weather, too, was not good."

hurriedly cutting them up and they were trying to dry them. Meanwhile some of the men were hunting. But they were most happy with the fish.

Really, everybody was working. For a while some of them were getting acquainted with different places. When they arrived they had found that Carta Bay wasn't far off from where they had landed, so they moved there. This is what they called Kasaan. But later they found Dog Salmon Creek. They named it for what the raven used to say. They called it cháats. *And the place where they lived they called* chaats chúunii. *But now Eagle Creek is called Chomley.*

Now when fall fishing season comes there are lots of fish. They named the creek for the way the raven called. And then they settled at a place across from chaats chúunii *too.*

Their chief, their leader, I don't know what he died of. He died and they were living across from Small-water-that-flows, a place with good ground and beautiful scenery; it was there they buried the man. It is for him they named a small flowing creek but I don't know the name.

Since then, when they dry their fish they all move to the place they found. It was Kasaan. Now they call it "Old Kasaan." But it was back at that time that people first moved to Kasaan. The people were the Yaadaas Haida clan. My people are Yaadaas. From there they moved to New Kasaan but I don't know when.

The reason I'm telling you this is because of the struggle of the Yaadaas people. The muddy-mouth people moved when it was near summer. For this reason things were good for them. But when the Yaadaas people moved it was becoming fall. When the Yaadaas people moved it was such a struggle for them. The weather was so bad and cold but that's the reason I told you about when Raven saved them. The Raven saved them at that place they first called chaats chúunii. *When we tell stories in Haida they're not really specific. Our talk goes anywhere storytelling. And then because of the Raven, the Raven people's living conditions got nice. As white people say I will say to you folks—they didn't forget it and then, too, they always appreciate.*

Kasaan land was nice. Fish were plentiful. Deer were near there. At Carta Bay too, sockeye were near and plentiful. They made a good move, the Yaadaas people.

The welfare of the muddy-mouth people improved, too. The story wasn't much. But the place when they first found water was running, now that place is theirs; we call it Hedda Creek. It's the muddy-mouth people's water. The creek too belongs to them. But if others get fish from there the people don't resent it. The muddy-mouth people are always generous with their creek. They don't bicker about it. Others can take as much as they want.

My story is finished.

Contact between the Prince of Wales (Kaigani) and Queen Charlotte (Masset and Skidegate) Haida has continued down to the present through intermarriages, jointly held ceremonials and religious events, the mutual use of natural resources, and visiting. The Haida, to a great extent, remain a unified people and identify easily with the following narrative that was first told in the Skidegate dialect near the end of the prehistoric period.

In this narrative, the Ninstints people are depicted as having approached the Skidegate people for the purpose of a raid on the Bella Coola. They sought an alliance with a Skidegate group, the Kaisun. During the raid a number of Haida were killed. In this story the practice of capturing slaves is mentioned. We hear about war trophies such as an enemy's hair or blanket. This particular story of a raid is told in the first person and has to do with one man and his combat experiences. The war party was generally unsuccessful; it returned to Kaisun empty-handed. This fact in itself is indicative of the decline of the old ways of doing things. One can imagine that failed raids were not the stuff of *gyáehlingaay* a century earlier! Indeed, the narration here is more a factual account of a historical event than a story in any entertainment sense.

It is unfortunate that more of the context of this Skidegate story is not recoverable. Lillian Pettviel, in rendering it for us from English to Kaigani, was unaware of any of the events from her knowledge of Haida oral history. According to Krause (1885, as translated in Gunther 1956, p. 210), raids were undertaken by Haida to procure slaves. Commonly, Haida raided Tlingit territory to the north but, as this story shows, southern Haida would go on raids to the mainland as well. With contact, raids diminished and so did the availability of slaves. The Haida are known among Northwest Coast groups for regarding slaves as a "unit of value" in terms of currency. According to Krause, "A slave in Wrangell's time (ca. 1839) was worth twenty-five beaver skins or two sea otter skins" (p. 128). By 1885 the price of a slave had risen to two hundred woolen blankets (p. 210). Woolen blankets came to replace bark blankets as a unit of value once the Hudson's Bay Company went into production for trade.

John Swanton included this Skidegate text at the end of the Haida grammar he wrote for Franz Boas's *Handbook of American Indian Languages* (1911:277-81). It was presented in the phonetic orthography used by Swanton and other pioneering linguists including Boas himself. Swanton gave interlinear English translations with notes keyed to his grammar. A free English translation of the Skidegate text was given separately (pp. 281-82). That English translation is the basis of the Kaigani version presented here.

A Skidegate Raid on the Bella Coola

The Ninstints people came to Kaisun in four canoes to ask the people to go to war with them.[16] *Then they went along in four canoes. After they had crossed [to the mainland], they entered Bentinck arm. And they went in opposite the fort during the night. Then some people who had been camping in the inlet began firing from in front. There Amai'kuns was killed. They also wounded Floating. They also wounded Beloved. He was a brave man among them. There they also enslaved two persons. After that they started out. And those who started first went out to some people who were coming along under sail. The noise of two guns was heard. Afterwards the canoe drifted away empty, and they enslaved two women. The others came thither, and while they lay close to the land, rejoicing over the persons captured, some people came sailing around a point in a canoe, saw them, and jumped off. Then we landed in pursuit of them. And after I had spent some little time preparing myself, I got off. And I started to pursue one person who was running about near the sea. After I had chased him about in the woods for a while, he jumped into the ocean. And I took his hair, along with his yellow-cedar bark blanket, away from him. And he came up out at sea and held up his hands in front of my face (in token of surrender). Then he swam shoreward toward me.*

When he got near me he dove again and came to the surface out at sea, and I began to shoot at him. Then he swam landward and held himself tightly against the face of a certain cliff. After I had shot at him twice there, I stopped. Then he climbed up upon a tree standing upon the face of the cliff. And although its top was some distance from the cliff, he bent it toward it, and after a while got hold of the face of the cliff. And he went into a hole in it. He could not go from it either downward or upward. We said to one another that he would die right in it.

Then they started from that place in their canoes. Then they had a fire and began to give each other food. And after they again started off, they again began fighting with the fort. Then we got into a position from which we could not get away. Then, although we could not get away at first, they finally got us into the canoes. And a certain person crept around on top of the house. They shot him so that he fell down. And after they had lain out to sea for some time, a man wearing a dancing blanket and cedar bark rings dragged down a canoe and came out to us, accompanied by a woman. And those in Tldoogwaang's canoe talked to them. Then they told the woman to come closer, and said that they should shoot the man so that he would fall into the water. Tldoogwaang refused and started away from them.

---

[16] Because we have no firsthand knowledge of this raid we are reluctant to change the text to make it more readable; it appears here essentially as Swanton presented it (Swanton 1911:281-82). Unfortunately, the story is hard to follow in places, especially when it is unclear who "they," "he," and "we" are.

Then they fled away in terror. Their ammunition was all gone. Then we also started off.

Then they started from Point Djiidaao, and after they had spent four nights upon the sea, they came to Cape St. James. After they had traveled two more nights, they came to Kaisun. Instead of accomplishing what they had hoped, they returned from a far country almost empty-handed.

Here this story comes to an end.

Reminiscences

Even though much of the ethnographic record of the Haida has been lost, some idea of their cultural history may be gleaned from personal reminiscences of "the olden days." The Haida are fisherfolk and a hunting-and-gathering people. The first two reminiscences are a hypothetical and a real account of the celebration that generally took place when a young boy had his first successful hunting experience. These stories also provide a glimpse of the feasting process: the higher the status of the hunter, the bigger the festivity to celebrate the hunt. A "first kill" would trigger a potlatch preparation with dances, speeches, and elaborate food. The particular event recounted here is a spoof of a traditional potlatch. The old ways were being replaced by the new, but some sentiment for the way things used to be done was retained.

First Kill

A long time ago when a boy child first killed something, they honored him for it. They thought highly of him for killing any living thing. For killing any thing – deer, mink, seal – they celebrated with him because they thought so highly of it.

They invited everyone to celebrate. If he were a boy of high status they thought even more highly of him for the deed.

Depending on the occasion those living around the boy were the ones invited to celebrate. The people prepared a lot of food for his celebration. They thought as much of his event as of a potlatch. They danced while the food was being prepared and then they started to eat.

After the warmth of the food the time for ceremony arrives; they show off with the thing the small boy killed. That is the way they honored his deed. They "give him the day." That is what they call it.

"When my mother's brother was small he killed a small bird with a bow and arrow."

Mother's Brother's First Kill

When my mother's brother was small he killed a small bird with a bow and arrow. They invited just the people living around there at the time. After they danced and when they finished eating, they brought out his little bird on a pillow because they thought it was so cute. Once again they started dancing. That's the way my mother told me the story. That's all I have to say.

While boys gained prestige by bringing home meat, girls learned the importance of everyday gathering of seasonal berries and other vegetable material for both nutrition and dietary variety. "The Scaredest I've Ever Been in My Life" is a poignant account of the dangers inherent in the berry-picking task due to the threat of a bear attack. The narrative deals with a family affair prior to the onset of the main fishing season. As in the story of "Mother's Brother's First Kill," the cast of characters and circumstances of the event might have been different in the days before contact.

The Scaredest I've Ever Been in My Life

Long ago when they used to seine at Copper Mountain, families used to berrypick together. There was a creek across the bay from the cannery with a lot of berry bushes growing at the mouth of the creek. Also, there used to be a lot of bears at Copper Mountain. My parents used to go there often in the few days before they started fishing.

One day we went berrypicking. I thought they were hurrying for some reason. And then I was still a small child but I used to be a good berrypicker.

When we went there berrypicking it was getting close to evening, we really picked berries in a hurry! There were many bear droppings around there. Really, I was scared to death! I was picking berries just any old way. I really thought I would die of fright! I was so frightened of the bears I thought I'd die.

I used to think about my experience. I never asked my parents about it or told them how scared I was. After that I used to be scared of any bears.

How we got back to the cannery, I don't remember. But if I didn't live through it, I couldn't be telling you about it now!

There's no more to my story. Thank you.

In the Skidegate story of the attack on a Bella Coola village, we see examples of Haida calling people by names that refer to their physical qualities. The names *giitlagún* and *kwiiáas* translate as "floating" and "beloved," respectively. No translation is given for *amai'kuns*, but it is tempting to speculate that it may be a loan nickname for "American" with the "s" appended for grammatical reasons.[17] Krause (1956:210) recounts the precontact naming practice whereby "the first-born son usually receives the name of the mother's brother, the second child that of the next brother or another name of the eldest brother. If there are no brothers, the name of a friend is chosen or the name of the one whose spirit is reincarnated in the newborn child according to the shaman." This naming practice brings out the important role of the mother's brother in Haida society. Again, in "The First Kill," members of the mother's clan planned and prepared the festivities. Traditionally, a youth would take a new name from his mother's relatives as many as four different times as he grew to adulthood. Today, children are seldom named specifically for their mother's eldest brother; instead, a close female relative might dream about one of the child's ancestors a few days before the birth. The child may be given the name of that ancestor, either officially or off the record. The child is then thought to be born with many of the personality characteristics of the ancestor who figured in the dream.[18]

It remains the case that most people (men and women) are referred to by various nicknames. "Paul's Name" recounts how the nickname given to one child in fun resulted in his being awarded a "real Haida name" by a woman who had the authority to bestow it. The little boy's nickname started out as a derogatory statement referring to his physique and became a "real high-class name." But often, to the uninitiated, any given nickname seems to have little in common with the quality of the person or name it represents. In a community of Haida speakers, members "generally use a person's given name if that person is an outsider, otherwise a community nickname is used. . . . [N]icknames are of the type 'Fatty' for a person not fat, 'Aunty' for a person not related to the speaker, 'Toodles' for a respected town elder whose real name might be Chauncy. No one may know why they call Gertrude 'Dolly' anymore . . . " (Eastman 1985:12-13). People often have a Haida name, Haida or English nickname(s), Christian first and last names, and names representing clan and moiety affiliations.

Among a number of native peoples on the Northwest Coast, it was and is common to address both children and adults by nicknames denoting certain physical or behavioral characteristics (often whether the person so named exhibits these characteristics or not). Among the Twana, observed by Thompson (1985), nicknames might even be borrowed from the languages of

---

[17]-s is commonly used as a subordinate clause marker (Eastman and Edwards 1980). It can be appended to a single term to indicate its role as a subordinate or dependent clause. In this case *amai'kuns* would be interpreted as "the one who is American."

[18]This is a common belief among North American natives.

other neighboring Salishan groups, especially if the nicknamed person has ties with the name-giving group. A Twana man with the Christian name Henry Allen was called *qwaayak'*, a Klallam name meaning "laughing face." Allen's older brother, whose Christian name was Frank, was referred to as *hlumiichad*, a Twana proper name. Their niece was given the Klallam nickname *xwaxwang*, "crybaby," as well as the Christian name of Louise. Twana proper names such as *hlumiichad* were given when people reached maturity and were used thereafter only during ceremonies. At other times adults were referred to by kin terms, other relational terms such as "companion," or in recent times by Christian names.

Nicknaming functions such that both the people with the license to use nicknames (and the cultural background to interpret and understand them) and those who receive them are core members of a particular society. Nicknames are acquired as people acquire membership in a group, at a late stage in the process of developing a group's social identity (see Eastman 1985). For social anthropologists, receiving a name is often a tangible sign of being accepted by or adopted into a group with whom they have been working. In Christian religions, name-changing is often a part of puberty rites (e.g., at confirmation). Name-changing is also a part of the process of becoming close in personal relationships. People in love use "pet" names, and friends have special names for each other. The culturally biased nature of nicknaming also functions in such a way that there need be no obvious relationship among a person's real or nickname. Among Kaigani Haida, people are even nicknamed for physical characteristics they do not possess—for example, a particularly hairy individual may be called "Baldy." In the story "Paul's Name," we see how Paul acquired the high-class name *kwaay íiwaans* "big flowing (stream)" which just happens to also mean "big butt."

Paul's Name

When my son Paul was this small his hips were this big but his legs were this big around. He was very short and fat. And then when Puuji and his friends came from the schoolhouse the children used to look at him. At that time "Big Butt" is the name we gave him. One time when Mrs. Davis was visiting mother we were making fun of him, calling him "Big Butt." "That name of his is high class, I give him the name," Mrs. Davis said. "It's a big name, 'kwaay íiwaans.' 'kwahgaay íiwaans' is the way you pronounce it." And so, you see, it's not our clan name. Mrs. Davis gave it to Paul. "It's really a true name," she said, when she gave it to him. "This is his name, 'kwaay íiwaans.'"

Western Forms: A Psalm and a Recipe

Both traditions and reminiscences as presented here clearly indicate ongoing cultural change. A raid on the neighbors no longer brings vengeful retaliation. The first kill is now a tiny bird rather than a fierce bear or elusive deer, and the celebration of the kill is more fun than ceremony; berry-picking takes place on the eve of a cash-producing economic activity (fishing).

Other cultural change included the introduction of Christianity and along with it, literacy in English. Early in this century, the residents of three villages on Prince of Wales Island embraced Christianity and built a new village, modeled on the American dream. Anticipating the future, these Kaigani pledged to forsake their former cultural and religious activities in exchange for a church and minister from a Presbyterian mission center in the "lower 48," that is, in mainland USA. Along with the new religion came opportunities to learn to read and write the English language; much of the church service required the use of English language prayer books and hymnals.

The first young Presbyterian minister at Howkan on Prince of Wales Island described his arrival as follows:

> How the wind howled up the strait between Dall Island and Long Island! (A) forest of totem poles greeted us when we rounded the point, scores of them, of all sizes and all of different shapes, from the tall eighty-foot pole which stood in front of *Skotlkah's* house, the brown bear pole surmounted by a finely carved image of a "Boston man" with stovepipe hat, to the little plain pole nine feet high on which was the single carved image of a killer whale. A flock of gulls screeched overhead, and the Native men and women, wrapped in their blankets, came from their houses to stare at us.
>
> As we came down the beach we saw thick black smoke pouring from the smoke-holes of a number of houses. We knew what that meant, and that in those houses stills for making hooch were operating full-blast; we knew also that at the foot of many of those totem poles were buried the bodies of slaves who had been sacrificed to the spirit of the man in whose memory the new house had been erected. We heard the tom-toms beating, and singing going on, in several houses, and two or three medicine-men came out to stare suspiciously at us as we landed in front of the chief's house. (Young 1927:237)

Today all Haida villages on Prince of Wales Island have been consolidated in the town of Hydaburg (see map 3, p. 28), under the auspices of the Presbyterian church. Most Haida are literate in English and many attended

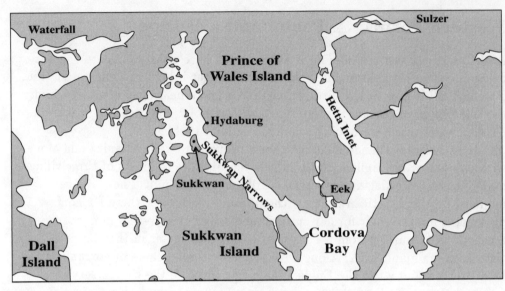

Map 3: Hydaburg

the then Presbyterian Sheldon Jackson Boarding School in Sitka, Alaska, or now go to both primary and high school in Hydaburg. Despite this, people who still know the Haida language may, from time to time, render their prayers and passages from the Bible into Haida.

Life in Hydaburg often involves activities in and around the church. Attached to the church itself is a hall with kitchen facilities where various social activities are held and Sunday School classes given. One of the most popular items at public events such as bake sales, the Fourth of July celebration, or Bingo (held usually at the Alaska Native Brother/Sisterhood Hall rather than the church hall) is communally prepared fried bread. We expressed interest in learning how to make fried bread and asked for the "recipe" forgetting that recipes, like psalms, are not indigenous forms of narrative expression. Both psalms and recipes are perceived as written forms of expression—seen primarily in the Bible and cookbooks, respectively. Initially, so that we could actually make fried bread, we were given an English-style recipe. That is, we were given a list of ingredients, were told what to do with the ingredients in order, and also received serving suggestions. However, when we were given the recipe in Haida, and when Psalm 46 was recited to us in Haida, an interesting transformation from written-English style to oral Haida took place. Both the psalm and the recipe, orally, took on the characteristics of *gyáehlingaay*, that is, they conformed to the usual structure of Haida narrative.

In the psalm we initially see a struggle to maintain a sense of the biblical language despite the fact that the words in English offer no easy translation into Haida. The first line, "God is with us," is especially troublesome. In Haida, the way to convey the oneness of spirit and person intended here is to say "we are two."[19] The next line, "God is our shelter and our strength," is also difficult since the association of shelter and strength in Haida is not as clear as it may be in English. The result in Haida is "with him we are saved." Part of the third line, "in times of trouble," is assumed from context in Haida and so is not explicitly stated.

The Biblical images borrowed into Haida via the King James Bible are often evoked through the use of complex verb phrases where English might use a predicate adjective construction (Eastman and Edwards 1985). This is as much a reflection of the different grammatical structures of Haida and English as it is an indication of the way the psalm lends itself to interpretation in the Haida language. In this psalm, as in Haida narratives in general, conjunctions are used to move things along. We see *wáadluu* ("and then") used in the psalm. It is translated as "so" but means here that "as a consequence of God being with us, as our shelter and strength and always ready to help (so) we don't need to be afraid."[20]

Another conjunction, *uugyaen* ("and") cements phrases within sentences while *asgáay(st)* ("after that") summarizes sequences of thought much the same way *wáadluu* ("and then") does. These particles and conjunctions preserve the flow of thought for listeners where punctuation and placement on the page would serve for readers.

A benediction is appended to the psalm, added by the narrator to provide a sense of dignity to the piece. This also makes the psalm especially "Haida."

Psalm 46: God Is with Us

God is our shelter and our strength.
   Always ready to help in times of trouble.
   So we will not be afraid.

---

[19] The way to express "We are two" in Haida involves using an intransitivizing particle *ga-* before the adjective *stang* "two." *ga-* makes the adjective "two" a verb. So *hiitl' ga-stáng* literally means "we two-become" (or "we become a single two-ness" in English). In Haida one can say *chíin uu hl táagan* ("I eat fish") using the object *chíin* ("fish"), or one can say *hl ga-táa* ("I eat" or "I become an eater"), where the absence of *chíin* necessitates the use of the intransitivizing particle *ga-* before the verb stem *taa* ("eat").

[20] *wáadluu* usually has the function of breaking a narrative into sections so that what follows is a consequence of what went before. Its communicative function is to involve the listeners in the progress of the story and to signal that a change in activity or point of view is taking place. In the psalm, *wáadluu* indicates that the content of what went before taken together adds up to our not needing to fear.

Even if the earth is shaken and the mountains too, even if they fall into the ocean depths we will not be afraid. No matter how much the seas roll and how much the seas throw things into a rage like the sound of the hills shaking, even then we will not be afraid.

There is a river that brings joy to God and to God's sacred house. God is in that city. No matter what happens his city could not be destroyed. In the early dawn he'll help the river, the earth will be terrified, kingdoms too are shaken. God thunders and the earth goes up in flames. God's mighty self is one with us.

We are safe with Jacob's father. Come, see what God has done! What amazing things he finished on earth! He stops wars all over the land. He snaps bows and destroys spears. He lets shields burn up. "Stop fighting!" is what he said. But I myself, God himself, ourselves know all the time he is supreme above nations, supreme above the world. God Almighty is one with us. The God of Jacob is our refuge.[21]

This is the end of the scripture.

Thank you. Thank you. I thank you. Thank you. I pray that the Lord will bless us twofold. Thank you.

It was not until quite a while after we had a recipe for fried bread that we realized that just as we didn't have the same psalm in Haida that we have in English, the recipe is also different in the two languages. We find it revealing that in English we say we "give" a recipe while in Haida a recipe is "told."

The Haida recipe for fried bread may be seen in two parts. The first twelve lines tell audience members what the narrator feels they already know. This shared knowledge accounts for what happens in ordinary bread-making. The verbs, for the most part, are in the past tense. The part of the recipe that actually has to do with *fried* bread (not just the dough preparation that would be the same for any bread) consists of four four-line verses (sixteen lines).[22] In this section, verbs are inflected in the future tense and the conjunction *áajii* ("and then") links verse-internal matter in much the same way as *asgaay(st)* ("after that") does in the psalm. Each verse ends with a fully inflected verb giving the verses the character of utterances conveying complete thoughts. This structural principle explains the otherwise redundant lines 12 and 28. They are necessary to preserve the four-line narrative pattern.

---

[21] This is how the Psalm sounds after being translated into Haida and back into colloquial English.

[22] The division of the recipe into lines and verses follows the suggestion of Hymes (1981) and is shown in detail on pages 90-92. Attention to pauses, the use of particles and conjunctions, and the way the narrator blocks out chunks of Haida to translate provide clues as to the way the narrative is organized.

How to Make Fried Bread

When you are going to make bread
you measure your flour for it.
Water and salt and sugar
they stir together.

You warm the milk,
you measure about 5 cups of flour.
About two spoons of sugar, too.
Three teaspoons of salt.
Two big spoonfuls of oil.

About 3 cakes of yeast
into about a cup of water is fine.

Sugar, salt, oil into this bread.

Stir this whole thing together.
And then you knead.
And then you rub oil on it,
and then let it rise once.

After it rises you cut it in pieces.
Put it into 4 bread pans
and then let it rise once again.
Bake it about 45 minutes.

Save one loaf of dough.
Let some oil get hot in a frying pan.
And the bread, you will cut in pieces and fry in it.
When it is brown you turn it over in the skillet.

When it is fried you will dip it in sweet syrup
which you have poured into a small dish.
And after that, you drink coffee.
And you will be full.

When we were being told the recipe narrative in Haida, it seemed full of superfluous information, so we asked if there was a "fast" version we could use to make our bread in a hurry. What we got as the fast version was only three lines shorter than this version. What was striking, however, was that the fast version lacked any of the marks of Haida narrative structure. The contextualizing cues (*wáadluaan, áajii, asgáayst*) were missing, verses could not be readily identified, and there was no sense of four-line utterance structures ending in fully inflected verbs. Without these structural markers (left out supposedly to hurry along the telling of the recipe) the information comes across as a list, rather like the kind of recipes exchanged in suburban American settings. When it comes to frying the bread, as distinct from making loaves of bread, only one line was devoted to the process. But even the forced, fast version ended formulaically with "yours will be good," which compares structurally with the end of the recipe narrative "and you will be full." This may be an indication of the hold the unconscious structure of oral narrative has on native speakers—using a proper closing even when attempting to give a recipe rather than tell a story.

Formulaic aspects of narrative will also be seen in the final section in which we present three Haida tales. Tales often start with, "I'm going to tell you a story," and end with "That's all I have to say. Thank you," as does the Psalm. In the tales you will see *wáadluu* used throughout to connect episodes and *esgáayst* used as a wrap-up signal before the final bit of action.

Tales

Haida mythological beliefs survive in tales. These have been characterized by Haida artist Bill Reid as involving "a good selection of bestiality, adultery, violence, thievery, and assault," and ranging in richness from "bawdy yet profound tales of the trickster Raven to poignant, imagistic narratives of love and its complications in a world where animals speak, dreams come real, and demigods, monsters, and men live side by side."[23]

Two raven tales presented here illustrate the role of Raven in organizing the human world. In "Raven Finds Water," we see how clever Raven was in being able to find water that had been hidden by Island Spirit, and in returning it to the land that later would be inhabited by the Haida. (Centuries later, in the Kaigani account of the migration from Masset, we again meet Raven in the role of provider when he shows the *yáadaas* Haida where to get fish.)

Raven Finds Water

This story is called "Raven Finds Water."

A long time ago, they say, the water dried up. There wasn't any anywhere. And then all the small streams dried up too.

---

[23] From the book jacket of *The Raven Steals the Light*, Reid and Bringhurst 1984. The reader is referred to this book, which contains a number of tales in English not presented here.

There was nothing anyone could do about it. They didn't know what to do. There was nothing that could be done for the people.

But Raven himself, feeling confident, got himself ready to do something about it. He would look for the water.

And then Raven knows it is the Island Spirit at Hazy Island that owns the water. But no one else knows where the water is. Only the Island Spirit knows.

And then Raven took a canoe to go to the island. He started out toward the island on a canoe.

He got himself ready to steal the water from the Island Spirit as he rowed himself toward the island. When he got halfway there the fog blew in and covered him. And then when the fog densed up too much, he was lost. And then he was just floating around there.

Raven was wondering what he could do about it.

When the Island Spirit found him there this is what he said to him: "You shouldn't be here. There's nothing here for you. Nothing. The weather will handicap you. There isn't water on the island."

This is what he told Raven.

He also said to him, "Don't be crazy! Turn back, back, turn back!"

This is what he would tell him.

And then Island Spirit left him.

Raven pretended he was going back. But it wasn't long afterward that he turned back again toward Island Spirit's home. He used the sun to get his bearing. He rowed according to it. While he was rowing he heard the surf. Soon he heard the surf breaking on the island.

He arrived at an inlet on the beach and the Island Spirit welcomed him. He came to meet him on the beach. Because he was so glad to see him he invited him to his home.

And then Raven acted as if he was thirsty. He exaggerated how thirsty he was.

The Island Spirit had hidden the water. He really made sure his water was hidden.

Raven was curious about it. And then, because he had a strong mind, he was able to stay there with him for a long time in spite of his thirst. He was looking for Island Spirit's water. He was wishing he could find where the water was hidden, looking at Island Spirit suspiciously.

(Speaker sings in a high monotone:) waited for him—waited for—

He waited for him.

In the meantime he thought about how he could get the best of Island Spirit. He wanted the water so badly. He wondered about it for a long time when suddenly, by chance, the Island Spirit got tired. So while warming his back at the fire he went to sleep!

And then while he was sleeping, Raven went towards a rookery-cliff, scooped up quite a bit of bird droppings and went back to Island Spirit while he was sleeping and rubbed it (the droppings) all over his (Island Spirit's) clothes. And it was after that Island Spirit woke up.

And then Raven said to him, "You stink really bad. You stink really bad."

And then the Island Spirit thought he had made himself stink. It was because he had been looking for eggs. While he was looking for eggs, he had made himself stinky, he thought.

And so Raven said to him, "do bathe yourself, do bathe yourself."

And then Island Spirit made himself ready. He got himself ready to bathe. He got his basket ready for the water and he left. He went to get water. While he was confused he forgot that he had lied to the Raven. He had said that there was no water to be found.

And after that he walked quite a ways from the house. There was floating moss hanging from the rock and ground swells breaking there below. Under the hanging moss was the water hole.

And thus Raven discovered where the water was and he prepared to steal the water. He would steal from the Island Spirit.

And then when early morning came he sneaked out from his house. He took his water basket and walked to where the water hole was. And because he was thirsty he drank water for a long time. He was very thirsty. He took a long drink.

Afterwards he filled up his water basket. He filled his beak too. And then after he got all the water he could he flew toward where the big island was situated. Still water was not to be seen there.

And then Raven, while flying around high over the land, he sprayed the water from his nose. Where water once flowed he blew water and he blew it onto the land. While he was doing this he was blowing water even into the middle of the clouds.

While this was happening it started raining and it didn't stop. And then where the water used to flow it got full. Flood flowed.

(Speaker chants:) the creeks crested—

After that, water was plentiful and the people were happy. And it was Raven, they said, Raven saved the country.

This is the end of my story.

"The Octopus Story" explores the interaction of humans with mythical beings of the sea. It makes reference to the carving ability of the people and is set at Hydaburg Creek in Southeast Alaska. Several supernatural events take place in this story: a woman is captured by the Octopus people and lives with them under the water; the Indian Doctor can "see" what is going on in the underwater village of the Octopus people; the Octopus child changes himself to human form to visit his grandparents. Descriptions of ideal Haida behavior include the way parents instruct their children by talking to them, the response of the village to the disappearance of the woman and their subsequent acceptance of the fact, and the magnanimity of the Haida chief once the enemy's evil plan does not succeed. Even though the children disobey their parents' injunction, the revenge plotted by the Octopus people is too severe and they are overcome by the wit of the Indian Doctor and the courage of the members of Brown Bear House.

The Octopus Story

A long time ago when the Haidas would tell stories they always included the story about the Octopus. Their village was there at Hydaburg Creek north of North Pass. There were over a thousand people that lived there.

My uncle, Saa Duutsaa, made an octopus "image" carving about his totem. His pole was at North Pass years ago.

Back then the Haidas taught their children many things. Many things were taboo. They put a lot of fear into their children about a lot of things. They made them respect everything. Their children should not abuse live things. "Be careful with them, you might be punished," they told the children.

The parents told them not to bother living creatures many times. They didn't talk that way because they were mean. They were careful with their children. They watched over them carefully. That's why they were strict with their children.

A long time ago people lived at North Pass continuously. And the Haidas, too, lived there generation after generation. There were many people of the Raven clan and a lot of Eagle clans there too. They lived there all together in peace. They didn't quarrel with each other. They never fought each other.

And so I have arrived at the beginning of the story.

One time a Raven woman took a canoe and rode away to look for roots. After she was gone for a while she didn't come back. Her people went to look for her and found only her empty canoe floating between islands across from where the village was.

It happened that an Indian Doctor knew something about her. He knew she was living in an octopus village under the water and that she was unable to return to her home. He knew that about her for a fact. Because the Raven people believed this story it eased their sorrow. It was like this for a while.

One day children were playing on the beach. One boy saw a baby octopus swimming along the ebbtide. He was trying to save himself among the rocks.

The day before, when it became dark, the baby octopus had changed himself to human form and gone to visit his grandparents. They didn't recognize him, they didn't even pay attention to him.

"Seeing the baby octopus they started playing with it."

Some children playing on the beach had some long sticks. With them they poked things. Seeing the baby octopus they started playing with it. They forgot their parents' instructions warning them not to do such things. They forgot, too, the instructions about things taboo that had been told to them. They tried to flip the baby octopus onto the beach. The octopus baby tried to get himself back into the water. He saved himself and went back to the octopus village.

What the children didn't know was that the octopus baby was the child of Raven Woman. When he got back to the octopus village the octopus people got excited. They became very angry over what the children had done to the octopus baby. The octopus people were going to ask for payment for what happened to their child. They made up their minds to take revenge on the people.

The Indian Doctor had a vision of what was going on. He told the people what the children had done and what the octopus people planned to do about it. And another thing, he saw that Raven Woman tried to warn the people. He told the village how it was going to be, that the octopus people were coming to fight the Raven people. They would spread themselves around Brown Bear House, the Raven people should get themselves ready.

The trouble the children made made them angry at them.

The Eagle people lived there too but the octopus people didn't pay attention to them.

The chief said to his own people to make themselves ready to fight. "The octopus people are demanding payment. We can't pay attention to what they want."

The Indian Doctor told them the way things would be and he told them to get themselves ready for it too. "Make your house secure! Seal the smoke hole too! When night comes they come to fight."

It was exactly like they said.

The octopus people came from the water onto the beach, towards the chief's house, and crawled up on top. They thought they would be able to suffocate the chief and the people.

Towards morning the octopus people found they couldn't do it. Instead of what they had planned they had to start back to the water because they couldn't be out of the water for a long time. The attack of the octopus people failed and the chief's house was saved.

To commemorate, the chief gave a big potlatch. And then the Raven people and the octopus people made up and they honored Raven Woman and the octopus baby too.

This is a Haida story.

My uncle, Saa Duuts, used to tell about it and also the things he used to carve. That's what this story is about. I heard about his carving long ago.

That's all of my story.

In the third tale we are told about *qaao qaao*, a raven-child of a raven-chief. Depicted in this narrative is another human who has access to the world of the animals, a person who in this case understands the language of the ravens. The chief of the ravens reaches a judicious solution to the impasse created when humans and ravens act without consideration for each other. The settlement is fair to both ravens and humans. This tale explains why, to this day, ravens do not bother the fish drying racks at Carta Bay.

The Story of *qaao qaao*, or Quoth the Raven, "Nevermore"

A long time ago something happened at Carta Bay. I'll tell you a story about it. It's about a raven.

When they dried fish the people used to all move there to dry their fish. Every fall they moved there as a group.

On a certain day they were working on the fish. When they started hanging their fish there, Raven, a particular raven, started stealing their fish. (There were always many ravens there.) And this raven, he was tricky. He was clever. He always got the best of them. He, stealing their fish, walking on top of them, he shredded them with his claws.

And so on a certain day a man said: "I'm gonna kill that raven." And then he took his bow and arrow and hid himself in the bushes. While he was in there, while he was sitting there, the raven flew in. The raven didn't see him hiding there.

He took careful aim and shot him.

And then not long afterwards the ravens all started flying in. Their talking was really something. It made them mad that the people shot one of the ravens.

The people didn't understand what the ravens were saying. But there was one person, he understood raven language. It was really an amazing thing, the understanding of raven language. So whatever happened he understood. Whatever the ravens say he understands.

Meanwhile there were getting to be more and more ravens there.

It was really crowded there across the creek. Because many of them mixed together they become disturbed.

As for the one-who-understood-raven-language, he listened to them and he understood whatever was going on. The reason why all the ravens were acting like they were angry was because it had been a noble raven.

The one-who-understands-raven-language understood whatever was said. The ravens were truly angry, the dead raven had been the child of a dignified one. He had been a rich man's child.

The one-who-understands-raven-language understood that the ravens were getting themselves especially angry because the boy had been a chief's child.

The bickering of the ravens increased. They were throwing the people's fish around. And so the people began to worry.

The understander-of-raven-language told them the reason for so many ravens being there. And then he told them this: "It is the case that the raven they shot is the chief's child. His name was qaao qaao."

And then indeed, the ravens sounded as if qaao qaao is what they said as they cried "they killed qaao qaao, they killed qaao qaao." The raven they killed is what the ravens were all calling about.

And then the people decided to pay for having killed the chief's child. They regretted what happened to him and so they started to talk about making up. "We will make up to the ravens," is what they said.

And then, they hung up all the fish, as many fish as possible, for the ravens. They began to try to dry fish and then they invited the chief raven.

The one-who-understands-raven-language told the people, "The chief will fly here." And then they waited for him.

They waited for him for a while. . . . The ravens said to wait for him, the chief will fly here.

When he comes close the ravens pass the word to them.

Just as they said, the raven chief arrived. The raven was the biggest possible. It was amazing how big he was and while ravens are usually black, he looked blue. When he sat there on the tree he looked so blue that it amazed them.

Meanwhile the ravens that were there across the creek cried out. They called, crying to themselves, "Here is the chief, here is the chief!"

They said it for a while. . . .

The big raven composed himself and started to fly to the fish and then the story is this:

When he flew down to the fish, he ate for a long time. As he continued to eat he filled himself up. When he was filled up to bursting he quit. And as the chief feasted he said this: "You killed my child. I will try to forget the killed one." (White people say it this way, "forgive.") "He really made a mistake in this deed, my child did, therefore he got killed. It's OK now, it's OK. I'll tell the raven people never to do this same thing after this and they will be good."

Afterwards he flew away.

And after he flew away, the ravens waiting for him across the creek all flew over here to the fish and they feasted. They all made themselves full and then they all flew away.

After that there were no more ravens and the people didn't fight among themselves.

The story I told you is true. It happened at Carta Bay.

My story is over.

Thank you.

Conclusion

In the preceding pages, we have presented a range of Haida narratives in such a way as to acquaint an unfamiliar reader with the language and the culture. At the same time, we hope that the way we have depicted the language in translation, and the appended ethnographic and linguistic notes, evoke familiar feelings among Northwest Coast native peoples who read the book.

No assumption has been made here that these *gyaehlingaay* are part of the repertoire of any group of people, yet their type and range, and their performance by Lillian Pettviel and a few other Kaigani Haida, may be seen as representative of a living oral tradition following almost a century of rapid cultural change and varied culture contact. The Skidegate story, which is retold in Kaigani, demonstrates starkly the gap that has developed between the Kaigani and Canadian Haida in the years since Swanton collected the Skidegate version in 1911. A number of the allusions in the story of the Skidegate people executing a raid on the Bella Coola are uninterpretable by Pettviel in the retelling. We can no longer account for the contextual meanings of the nicknames Floating, Beloved, and Amai'kuns. Because we do know that nicknaming is common in the Kaigani community today and that naming has a ritual and social bonding function among other Haida, we can conjecture that these particular Skidegate figures were highly valued community members.

Names of people and places are ways in which the routines of everyday behavior, which social scientists refer to as *social episodes*, are represented in the minds of people who interact with each other. When people of a particular society tell stories, they present a cognitive representation of the everyday social reality they share (Forgas 1979). These Kaigani *gyáehlingaay* as a group, despite their disparate form as historical narrative, reminiscence, tale, or translation of psalm and recipe, give us a sense of how one particular group's experience has been both retained and changed in a time of diverse multicultural contact and radical socioeconomic change.

The world of the Kaigani Haida that emerges in these pages is one characterized by fishing and boat building, berry picking in the woods, and ties to Masset and other Queen Charlotte Island locales. Wind and rain and cold come into play in nearly all events and activities. Raven was relied upon to call out various types of information that the people needed to know, ranging from weather watches and travel cues to how to behave appropriately, how to handle fish, and where to fish and hunt. The narratives reveal the workings of Kaigani clan structure (for example, the Octopus people were angry only at Ravens, not at Eagles), the way settlements were established on Prince of Wales Island in Southeast Alaska, and how the clans managed to live together. We catch a glimpse of a past in which slavery and scalping were factors, warfare and raids took place, and gunfire was rampant. Memories of dancing blankets and cedar bark costumes as used in the nineteenth century are evoked in the retold Skidegate raid narrative. Less distant reminiscences are brought out in the story of the little boy who came home in triumph after successfully bagging a bird during a hunt. This transformation from the days of fur trapping is set amidst an equally transformed potlatch—now a potluck. The story juxtaposing berry picking and bears with the cannery also reveals a contact context. The locale of the best berry-picking area, now referred to as "across the bay from the cannery," had previously been "the woods by the creek near the Copper mountain seining area."

The most obvious contact influence in these narratives is seen in the reformulation of Psalm 46 and the telling of a recipe in terms of Haida narrative structure. An interesting situation arises when an archaic English translation of a Latin translation of an Aramaic text is expressed in terms of Haida grammar and vocabulary. The psalm's translation also reveals the impact of Christianity on the Haida.

The recipe for fried bread told in story form is an example of the persistence of a Haida way of speaking despite the introduction of literacy, education, and various western modes of communicative presentation. The idea of recipes as literature is somewhat startling. Yet since recipes are known to have been passed down from generation to generation in most societies, the fact that they conform to the narrative structure associated with a particular culture ought not to be surprising. It would be interesting in modern, and for the most part literate, United States society to examine recipes and other forms of oral tradition still extant in order to discover what structural narrative features may exist that might be remnants of an early American folk narrative form. It is striking that such divergent forms of talk as reciting a psalm and telling a recipe lend themselves so readily to a *gyáehling* format.

The tales presented in the final section portray a sense of the traditional Kaigani belief system—the way in which Haida society works and what beliefs and expectations Kaigani people hold with regard to each other. Raven is depicted as the world's organizer—assuring the peoples' water supply and good fishing areas. Raven also intercedes on behalf of the people, often manipulating—even tricking—various spirits in the process. The Island Spirit is so muddled by Raven that it leads Raven right to the water it had said was nowhere to be found! The story of the octopus/human baby (born to a Raven woman who had been taken to an undersea octopus village) imparts the lesson that it is wrong to tease or disturb animals and fish. The ensuing attack on the land-dwelling people of the Raven clan by the octopus people from under the sea was foiled at its outset. By nature, octopus people cannot remain on land long enough to stage a siege against the Raven clan barricaded in their houses. Here is a clear example of human advantage over nature, coupled with the Haida's own desire to have peace between the two. Equilibrium is restored at the potlatch given by the chief of the Raven clan that includes the octopus people and honors Raven Woman and her octopus baby. The magical aspect of this tale requires us to suspend our belief regarding the ability of Raven Woman to live under the sea with the octopus people, and of the octopus people to stay on land long enough to attend a conciliatory potlatch but not long enough to win a small war.

Haida social control again is highlighted in the tale of the raven *qaao qaao*, killed for stealing the fish the people had been drying in the sun. The felicitous bridging of the gap between the people's world (culture) and that of the ravens (nature) by the person who understands raven language makes it possible for the people to know how angry the ravens are that one of their most valued group members has been killed. This conflict eventually is resolved when the people allow the Raven chief and other ravens to feast until full on the people's fish and when the chief, once sated, vows that ravens nevermore will interfere with the Haida's fish drying. To this day, the Haida dry their salmon in the sun at Carta Bay without fear of raven intrusion.

The attention we have paid to the Haida *gyáehlingaay* presented in these pages is intended to be in keeping with Dell Hymes's (1981) call for more works presenting and examining American Indian verbal art. In a survey of North Pacific Coast ethnopoetics, he included a translation and analysis of a Haida cradle song for boys extracted from Swanton's work on Haida in the Queen Charlotte Islands at the beginning of this century. With regard to verbal art in general, Hymes notes that:

> Linguistics and linguistic-like analyses are necessary means to the joy and understanding, because words were the means used by the authors of the texts. If we do not deal with the means, we cannot possess the meanings. . . . If we refuse to consider and interpret the surprising facts of device, design, and performance inherent in the words of the text, the Indians who made the texts, and those who preserved what they made, will have worked in vain. (1981:5)

Hymes considers the Haida cradle song primarily from the perspective of its structure of repetition and variation, changes in word order and accentuation. Readers interested in learning more about Haida expressive culture are referred to Hymes's work and the cradle song (Hymes 1981:4-5), to some references to Haida poetry in Day (1951), and to a record of Masset Haida songs recorded by J. Enrico.[24]

Hymes found that enjoying verbal art texts as literature does require some philological analysis "to establish and justify the form of the text." When the works are presented formally in accord with an analysis of their structure, native speakers "find such presentations easier to read and use." Other readers are slowed down sufficiently that they can "attend to shape and meaning as they [the stories] unfold" (1981:382). If non-Haida readers are willing to be so slowed in their reading of the English structures presented in these pages, we feel that a greater sense of the Kaigani *gyáehlingaay* will be conveyed. This is especially true with regard to the English in the two Raven tales and Octopus story. The formal progression of "Raven Finds Water," the "Octopus Story," and *"qaao qaao"* is inextricably entwined with their content. Repetition and word building are devices used to create particular moods, while different connectives and conjunctions serve to segment episodes and to let careful listeners know when plot change and resolution are about to take place. This manner of presenting the English translations results in less-than-perfect English grammar and style, but we feel that such translation reveals more of the Haida language's essence and contributes narrative suspense.

And now, in true Haida style, let us bring our own narrative to a close formulaically: *Áao tlaan gyáehlingaay Gíidang. Há'waa.* "Here our story ends. Thank you."

---

[24]Queen Charlotte Island Museum, Second Beach, Skidegate, Queen Charlotte, B.C., Canada.

Stories in Haida

The Migration from Masset (When the People Came North)

kasáan	aa	tl'	ch'áagitk[25]	tláagaans	gyaehlingaay uu	jíingaagan
Kasaan	to	they	move	first	story	long is

The-people-first-moved-to-Kasaan story is a long one.

k'ínits	dluu	cannerysgaay	tl'	ch'áag hit	xúust
summer	when	cannery	they	move	start

In the summertime everybody would start to move to the cannery.

yáadaas	xaatáay uu	guu	na áang	ii	tl'	tláagaangaan
Yaadaas	Haida	there	living	at	they	first

ikwaan	gam	áatlin	gyaehlingaay	gam	áajist	kúnstan
but	not	here	story	not	from here	point

**The Yaadaas Haida were the first ones living there but the story
doesn't start from here.**

wáa	kunáast	Gístluu	tadáay	Gístluu
that	from the point	how many	years	how many

q'wútaas xaatáay	xaatáay uu	Alaska	aa	ch'aak	tláagaangaan
muddy-mouth	people	Alaska	to	move	first

**Before that, how many years past, the *q'wtaas xaataay* people were the
first ones to move to Alaska.**

gyaehlingaay	yakkiiáagan
story	true is

This is a true story.

Masset	aehl	tl'	na áangs	dluu
Masset	at	they	living	when

q'wútaas xaatáay	gwa	ch'a uu gutáangaangaan
muddy-mouth people	there	starving

**When the people used to live in Masset the *q'wtaas xaataay* there were
starving.**

---

[25] *ch'áagitk* from *ch'aak; ch'aagáa,* "when you move from one place to another"; *ch'aagik,*
"the action of moving"; *tl' cháag hit tlaagaans,* "when they first started to move."

"Because they ate roots and bark, the area around their mouths was stained a muddy color."

xaadaas   k'álaat   tlaa   xadúu   na'áangs
Haidas   other   them   around   living
Gíiduu   q'wii xaatáas   xaatáay   an   tl'   gwadánggaangaan
down   muddy-mouth   people   toward   they   thought

Other Haidas that lived around them used to think lowly of the *q'wii xaataas* people.

gin haganáan   q'wii xaatáas   hin   tl'   kiáasii uu
reason   q'wii xaataas   this   they   called
díitsii   qáahlii   aa   uu   na'áanggaangaan
woods   inside   in   lived

The reason why they are called *q'wii xaataas* is they used to live in the woods.

tlaa   xadúu   gin   iináas dlaas   q'wúl   táagaangaan
them   around   things growing   roots   eat

They used to eat roots of the things that grew around them.

q'íidaay   q'uts q'álaasaan   k'wúl   tl'   táasii   hluu
tree   skin   roots   they   eat   because
xehlíi   xadúus [26] *ii   gin   kwadláangaa   gans gingáanuu   q'áenga*
mouth   around   things painted   like   looked

Because they eat roots (and) bark it looked like things were painted around the mouth.

gam   xaatgáay   ch'aagáay   láa'angaangaan
not   people   lived   good wasn't

The way the people lived wasn't pleasant.

gám tlák   chíin   isgyáen   gin   chíinaa
no way   fish   and   things fish
istáahlingei   q'áengga'anggaangaan
could get   seeing not

They couldn't see their way to get any fish or seafood.

---

[26] *k'wat xadúu* = around their lips

tlaa	*q'atgúust*	*dluu*	*gaa*	*na'áangs gaang*
them	out from	when	there	living

kún	*xaatáay*	*isgyaen*	*káahlgwaa*	*xaatáay*	*waa*	*xaat*
point	people	and	inside	people	there	people

xaatáays	*gam*	*q'wii xaatáas*	*háwaan íntgangaangaa*[27]
people	not	muddy-mouth people	go fishing

Those that lived on the outside of them, those that lived at the point and those that lived in the cove, those people wouldn't (let) the *q'wii xataas* go fishing.

waagyáen	*sanáan*	*tlaa*	*t'alk*	*qing*[28]	*gans gingáan uu*
and then	too	them	against	see	like

q'wii xaatáay		*an*	*tl'*	*gwadánggaangaan*
muddy-mouth people		toward	they	thought

And then too, they thought of the *q'wii xaataay* just like they had hatred in their faces for them.

gut án	*tl'*	*Gaayhlgíi gaangaan*	*tl'*	*súugan*
together	they	fight	they	say

They say they used to fight amongst themselves.

q'wii xaatáay		*Gii Gáagahl*	*gyaen uu*
muddy-mouth people		fed up	and

waa	*saagúust*	*tlak*	*kún*	*tl'*	*qiinsii*	*aa uu*	*tl'*	*kasáasdlaayaan*
there	north	land	point	they	seeing	there	they	leave readied

The *q'wii xaataay* got fed up with the conditions and seeing a point of land to the north of them they got ready to leave to there.

waast	*júngaagan*
from there	far was

It was a long ways from there.

singaay	*laas*	*dluu*	*sGúnaan uu*	*tlagáay*	*qáenggagaangaan*
weather	nice	when	only	land	visible was

When the weather was nice was the only time the land was visible.

---

[28] *t'alk qing* = to have something against someone (*[lit]* to see by comparison)

wáadluu	*jíingaas*	*an*	*tl'*	*wúnsits*	*gyaenaan uu*
and then	far	to	they	knew	if
tlak	*Giduuwáanuu*	*tlakw*	*na'áangs*	*t'álguu*	
whatever	would be	whatever	living	in comparison	
tl'	*ch'áagaay*	*láa'asaan*	*tl'*	*gwadáns*	*dluu*
their	lives	good would be	they	thought	when
Gáa	*tl'*	*qasáa*	*asdláayaan*		
it	they	go to	readied		

Even if they had known it was a long way from there, no matter what, any kind of living (would be) better; they thought their living conditions would be good as they got ready to move.

ch'aagei'an	*an*	*tl'*	*Giihldaayaan*
moving to	selves	they	prepared

They got themselves ready to move.

xaatgáay	*ii*	*kíngaa*	*tláagans*	*dluu*
people	to	news	first	when
tl'	*gudingaay*	*hlkwiid*[29]	*isdláayaan*	
they	minds	moving	became	

When the people first heard the news they got all excited.

sínuu	*q'wíitaas*	*xatáay*	*Xáajaa uu*	*tl'*	*ga kíhlaas*[30]	
what	muddy mouth	people	do	they	plan	

What are the *q'wii xaataas* people up to?

sintlaa	*tlíi*	*tlúu*	*tl'*	*tlaaóhlaan*	*sinuu*	*tl'*	*xajáaohl*
why	many	boats	they	make	what	they	do

Why are they making so many boats? What are they up to?

hingáan uu	*tláa*	*tl'*	*tla-q'aldángs*	*gyaen*	
really		them	they	made amazed	and
xaatgáay	*tl'áa*	*xadúu*	*na'áangs;*		
people	them	around	living		
gudingáay	*tla-hlkwii*	*kyáenaan uu*	*gam*		
minds	made worried	even though	not		
tleihl	*tl'*	*kyáananganggaanaan*			
them	they	asked			

They just had them (the neighbors) amazed and the people living around them, even though they were worried, they didn't ask them.

---

[29] gudingaa hlkwiid(aa) = you're worried, apprehensive

[30] *sinuu tl' ga kíhlwaa* = I wonder what their plans are; *hinuu hl gwadángan* = this is the way I'm thinking; *k'waa t'lang ga kíhlaas* = (say,) let's make plans

kíhlk   xáadaan uu   an   tl'   tla-Giihlgiidaayaan
talking   lacking   selves   they   made ready
Without talking they made themselves ready.

tla-Giihlgiis   dluu   clan-gaay   waadluaan uu   k'aasáa'asdláayaan
ready   when   clan   all   leave readied
When they were all ready the whole clan packed to leave.

wáasalíaao   xaatgáay   gwu   na'áangsii   ii   kingáagan
afterwards   people   there   living   to   news did
Afterwards the people living there got the news.

gam   tlákw   gyaehlingaay   an   tl'   wúnsitgahlaangaan
not   whatever   the story   selves   they   knew
gam   hán   díi   wúnsitang
not   any   I   don't know
How they got the story I don't know.

ikwaan   sahgúust   tlak   kún   tl'   qíns áa   xwu-istíits
but   north   land   point   they   see to   sailed
But they left sailing to a point up north they could see.

sGúnaanuu   Gan   tl'   wúnsitdaan
only   that   they   knew
That's all they knew.

waast   ámjuwaan   Gíistluu   sihlgáang   gyaahlán   tl'   gwadáangaan
far   while   when   back   story   they   heard
q'wii xaatáas   xaatáay   ch'aagáay   láasii
muddy-mouth   people   place   good
**Quite a while after it happened they heard the returning news that
the *q'wii xaataas* people's living conditions are good.**

tawaays   tlaa   an   kwaans
food   them   for   lots
Food is plentiful for them.

gin   waadluaan uu   tláa   an   duungáasii
things   all   them   for   close
Everything is close at hand for them.

Masset   díit   áa   tl'   na'áangsii   tl'   ch'aao   gutáanggaangaan
Masset   woods   in   they   lived   their   conditions bad
ii láa uu   wed   tl'   Gíidang
but   now   they   condition (changed)
**Their really poor conditions living up the woods from Masset now
were different.**

díaanuu   tl'   útlaagudáa   gans   gingáan uu
really   they   wealthy   like
gin   wáadlaa uu   tláa   án   duungáas   tláa   an   kwáan
things   all   them   for   close by   them   for   much
**Really, just like they're well off; all things are right at hand for
them, plentiful for them.**

gyaehlingaay   sihlgaang   tlaa   aa   stíihls   dluu   haósanaan
story   back   them   to   began   when   once again
Gáao   xaatáay   t'uts   qasáa'asdláayaan
bay   people   some   leave readied
**When the news flashed back to them once again some of the Masset
(bay) people got ready to leave.**

uugyaen   tlíistdluu   q'wii xaatáas   xaatáay   ch'aa   tláagaangaan
and then   just when   muddy-mouth   the people   moved   first
ga   tl'   q'úsgadaan
it   they   forgot
And then they forgot just when the *q'wii xaataas* people first moved.

sgyáenaan uu   an   tl'   tla-Gúhldaal
then even   selves they   got ready
But even then they got everyone ready.

an   tl'   tla-Gúhl   tluuwáays   áa   tl'   tla-Gúhldaal
selves   they   prepared   boats   for   they   prepared
They got boats ready one after the other.

táawaay   sanáan   áa[31]   *tl'   tla-Gúhlt*
food   too   theirs   they   made ready
They got their food ready too.

júngaas   ansa'áas   an   tl'   wúnsits   dluu
far   will be   selves they   knew   so
tlii uu   táauu   tl'   tla-Gúhldaayaan
much   food   they   made ready
**They know it's going to be a long trip so they prepared quite a bit
of food.**

waa   tlíi   an uu   tl'   Gúhlgiis   gyaen   tl'   xwu-istíidaana
there   much   for   they   ready   and   they   sail started
At last they were ready and they started sailing away.

---

[31] *áa < áangaa,* "their own"

íkwaan uu   tláak   wáajaagangaangaan
but   to them   hard time
But they had a hard time.

taajuuwáay   chis   gyáen
wind   severe and
The wind was blowing severely.

singáay   sanáan   gam   láa'ang
weather   too   not   good wasn't
The weather too was not good.

singáays   daGangáas   gwaan
weather   rotten   really
The weather was really bad.

gyáa qat   tláak   xwu-waajaangaanda
once in a while to them   wind hard time was
Once in a while the wind gave them a hard time.

xwu-istáalgaan   dáanuu   tlagáayk   tl'   dungéils   dluu
sail go along   a while   to land   they   close   when
gam   tlíijaan   hiikíi   tl'   is   an   tl'   wúnsitaangaan
not   where   exactly   they   were   selves they   knew didn't
íkwaan   tlagáay   dungéils   gingaan uu   Gaa   tl'   tluu   istíidaan
but   land   close   like   it   they   boat   went
After they sailed a long time, when they were near to the land, they didn't know exactly where they were but near land, they went to it rowing.

huugwaa   íntaang kwún   Gitkw   táajaas guu   tl'   Gasgwadáan
truly   Cape Chacon   down   beach   they   landed
Here at Cape Chacon down on the sand they landed.

gam   k'íigaanii   aehl   tl'   isáangaan
not   Kaigani   at   they   weren't
They weren't at Kaigani.

Cape Chacon   hínuu   wed   tl'   kyáat
Cape Chacon   is what now   they   call
Now they call it Cape Chacon.

Spanish xaatáay   gwu   istlaa'áayaan   dluu
Spanish people   there arrived   when
xáataas   hinuu   tl'   kyaatgan   Cape Chacon
Haida   what   they   call   Cape Chacon
When the Spanish arrived there the Haida called it Cape Chacon.

xáadaas   laast   sgatáayaan   gingáan uu   tl'   kyaatgáangaan
Haida   them from   learned   like   they   pronounce
The Haida pronounced it exactly as they learned it from them.

Cape Chacon   sagúust   duu   tl'   na'áang-idaan
Cape Chacon   north   is where   they   living started
íkwaan   singáay   daGangáas   gwaan
but   weather   bad   really
**They started living up north of Cape Chacon but the weather was
really bad.**

taajawáays   waak   chis   gwaan
wind   there   severe   really
The wind there was very stormy.

Masset aehl   Gíidaangaan   gingaan   qat guusthli   na'áangan   gingaan uu
Masset at   condition   like   ocean side   living   like
It was like living at Masset, like living on the ocean side.

singáay   tlaan   síngiits   jihlíist   dluu   tl'   t'íits   diáng
weather   them   tough   really   when   they   some   look for
íntgaangaan   tlak   k'álaat   aa   tl'   ch'áak aeng
went out   place   other   to   they   move
**When the weather was too tough for them, some of them went out
looking (so they could) move to another place.**

tl'   diáng   ch'aadáng   kaod
they   look for   moving   . a while
For a long while they looked, moving several times.

sihlgáa   tl'   istlaa'áas   taajuuwáay   waak   chis   dluu
back   they   came   wind   there   severe   when
an   tl'   giáa   gans gingáan uu
selves   they   ran   like
**When they got back, the wind was so hard it was like they ran for
safety.**

Gándlaay   k'áahlii   aa   tl'   Gasgadáang
creek   inside   to   they   landed
They landed up the creek.

gam   kwaan   tl'   guláa'ans   gyáenaanuu   Gátuu   jahlíis   gyaen
not   much   they   liking   but   stormy   much   and
gwa'aa uu si   hl   tadastlíit
rain   with   cold became
**They didn't like it much but even then it was too stormy and it got
cold with rain.**

tl'   gudingaa   hlkwiíd
they   mind   moving
They were getting desperate.

waadluu   nagyaa   tl'   tlaaohl-iidaan
and then   their house they build started
And then they started building their house.

q'ildaay   ii   tl'   hlGángwul
trees   on they work
They're working on the trees.

q'ildaay   sanáan   tlagaay   ii   sanáan tl'   tlaskwún iit
trees   too   land   on too   they clear   start
The trees too and the land too they started clearing.

hlGaay kyúust   duu   naay,   nayáan,   áangaa
hurriedly   is how house house for theirs
tl'   tl'aaohl   gwadanggan   daanuu yáahl tl'aa sáa xitlaagaangaan
they build   tried   while   raven them over fly to
While they hurriedly tried to make their homes, Raven used to fly hither above them.

gyáak'it   singáay   l   xitláa'as isgyaen
once in a while in the morning he flies here and
tl'aa si'út   'l   xitgwáang
them above he flies round
Once in a while in the mornings he flies here and he'd fly around above them.

tl'aa si'út l   xitgwáans dluu tsáats, tsáats, tsáats
them above he fly around when tsaats, tsaats, tsaats
hinuu   l   súugaangaan
is what he called
When he flew around above them "*Tsaats, tsaats, tsaats,*" is what he'd call.

huu   tláan   gin   l   súutgaangaan
oh,   only   thing he said
That's the only thing he'd say.

tl'aa sii út l   xitgwáang   kaóduu
them over   he flew around a while
sihlgáang hawuns l   stílgaangaan
back   again   he returned
After he flew around above them repeatedly for some time once again he'd return.

"While they were hurrying to make their homes, Raven used to fly around above them."

gyáak'it   síngyaas   dluu   haósanaan   l   xitláas
once in a while   evening   when   once again   he   flew down
Once in a while when it's getting evening once again he'd fly down.

tliijiist uu   l   xitlaa'asgáangaan
where from   he   fly down
The way he came from he flew down.

yáa uu   haos   l   xitlaasgáangaan
same way   once again   he   flew down
The same way once again he flew down. (From the way he flew down, he flew down once again the same way.)

waadluu   haosanaan   tl'aa   si'út   l   xitgwáans   dluu
and then   once again   them   over   he   flew around   when
tsáats, tsáats, tsáats,—tsáats   hinuu   l   suutgaangaan
tsaats, tsaats, tsaats,—tsaats   is what   he   said
And then once again when he flew around above them, "Tsaats, tsaats, tsaats, —tsaats," is what he used to say.

díaan   léi   ii   tl'   q'ahl qiiaas   dluu
really   he   to   they   realized   when
sihlgáang   l   Gitlaasgáangaan   yaa áan uu
back   he   flying down   same
haos   l   stílgaangaan
once again   he   returned
When they really realized what he was doing (he flew back down the same way), once again he returned.

wáadluu   láak   tl'   an-gwúng iidaan
and then   him to they   wonder start
For this reason they started to be curious about him.

íhlansgaay   t'úts   láa   dlaa tlúukáaydaan[32]
men   some   him   running after
Some men went running after him.

káahl   gwaa   gingáan   tl'   Gús   dluu
cove   towards   like   they   arrived   when
Gantl   kwaayáans   an   tl'aa   Giditlaa'áayaan
water   flowing   at   theirs   arrived
When they got up towards the cove (they) arrived at their flowing water.

---

[32] *dlaa*, "after"; *tlúu*, "run"; *qáay-* "went"

yángkyaanuu   *chíinaay*   *Gándlaay*
truly (they are just astonished) fish   water
aa   *kwaans*   *gwaan*
in   a lot   really
Truly, there were really a lot of fish in the creek.

sk'uk   *aehluu*   *st'aagáas*   *gwaan uu*
dog salmon   with   full   really
yángkyaan   *tl'*   *gudingáay*   *hlkwiid*   *iséihluu*
truly   they   mind   moving   getting
It was so full with dog salmon they were really excited.

kwáan aan   *uu*   *t'íits*   *tluuwáay*   *gwii*   *dáangwaasgwaan*
any old way   is how   some   canoe   into   threw
They really threw some into the canoe any old way.

t'íits   *hansanaan*   *úhlansgaay*   *t'íits*   *hánsaanaan*   *táajaay*   *gwii*
some,   too   men   some   too   beach   onto
dáang uu   *tl'*   *gudingáay*   *qínsei*   *tl'*   *gudingáay*   *hlkwiidáa*   *stist*
threw   they   mind   seeing   they   mind   moving   because
**Some, too, some of the men too threw them onto the beach because
they were happy, they were excited.**

sihlgáangaan uu   *haosanaan*   *tluu*   *Gáts*   *gyaen*   *tlaa*   *an*   *tl'*   *hlGei*
back   once again   rowed   fast   and   them   to   they   called
Once again they rowed back fast and they called to them.

wáastáahluu   *tl'áa*   *salíiaa gá*   *ijáan*
in the meantime   those   behind   were
naay   *ii*   *hlGaay kyuust*   *aa*   *hlGangwalaas*   *gwaan*
house   in   hurriedly   at   worked hard   really
**In the meantime, those that are left behind in the house (they)
really worked hurriedly.**

taanaa-naay   *hansanaan uu*   *aa*   *tl'*   *tla-Gíihlt uu*
smoke house   too   theirs they   prepared
The smoke house too, they prepared theirs.

án   *hlkwiiduu,*   *án*   *hlkwiiduu*
self   hurry   self   hurry
Hurry yourselves, hurry yourselves!

taanaa-naay   *hl*   *áangaa*   *tla-Gíihldaal uu*
smoke house   (Imperative)   yours   finish start
Finish your smoke house as you go along!

chíinaa   kwáan-gan
fish   many are
There are many fish.

wáa   gingáan uu   waadluuaan uu
there like   everyone
jaatgáay   dánhllaan uu   hlGángwalaas   gwaan
women   too   working hard   really
As was said, they all, the women too, were working hard.

wáastáahluu   úhlansgaay   hánsanaan
in the meantime   the men   too
chíinaay   q'úhlang iidáan
fish   transporting started
In the meantime the men too started transporting the fish.

sk'ugáay   kwáans   gwáanuu   xung   l
dog salmon   many   really   fish   they
Gustliiéiuu Gii aa   tl'   hlGángwal
fast as could   they   worked
**There were really so many dog salmon; they were working on them
just as fast as they can go.**

aa   tl'   k'adáas   gyaen   aa   tl'   tla-Gíldahl   gwadáng
theirs they   cut   and   theirs they   dry   try
**They were hurriedly cutting theirs and they were trying to dry
them.**

wáastáahluu   úhlansgaay   t'úts   hánsanaan   q'áajuugáangaan
meanwhile   men   some   too   hunt did
Meanwhile some of the men too were hunting.

íkwaan   chíinaay   aehluu   tl'   gudingáay   láa   jahlíigaangaan
but   fish   with   they   minds   happy   most were
But they were most happy with the fish.

yángkyaan   tl'   wáadluuaan   hlGángwalgan
truly   they   all   work did
Really, everybody was working.

kaóduu   t'úts   hánsanaan   tlagáay   sqatjaadáng
for a while   some   too   land   explored
**For a while some of them too were getting acquainted with different
places.**

esgaayst duu   *Carta Bayst*   gam   jíngaa áng guu
after that   Carta Bay from   not   far wasn't
aa uu   tl'   ch'aagáayaan   esgáayuu
there   they   moved   after that

After that, Carta Bay wasn't far off (from) there, they moved to there after that.

kasáan   hinuu   tl'   kyaatdáayaan
Kasaan   is what   they   called (it)

This is what they called Kasaan.

íkwaan   wáasalíaa   sk'uk   Gándlaay   tl'   qayáan
but   after that   Dog Salmon Creek   they   found

But after that they found Dog Salmon Creek.

yáalaay   tluk   súugaangaan   hluu   tl'   kyaatdáayaan
raven   what   said   is what   they   called (it)

They named it for what the raven used to say.

cháats   hinuu   tl'   kyáat
chaats   is what   they   called

They called it this way—*chaats*.

uugyáen   tlagáaykw   tl'   naáangaan   hansanaan
and   place   they   lived   too
cháats ch'úunii   hinuu   tl'   kyaatdáayaan
Chaats Chuunii   is what   they   called (it)

And then at the place where they lived too, Chaats Chuunii is what they called it.

íkwaan   wéd   ch'áak   Gándlaay   chámlii   hínuu   wéd   kyaat
but   now   Eagle   Creek   Chomley   is what   now   called

But now Eagle Creek is called Chomley.

esgáay guu   wéd   fall fishing gaa   dluu   chínaay   kwáan-gangan
there   now   fall fishing   when   fish   lots are

Now when fall fishing season (is) there are lots of fish.

yáalaay   tlakw   kyaatdáayaan   hluu   tl'   kyaat
raven   whatever   called   is what   they   named (it)

They named it for the way the raven called it.

uugyaen   ch'aats chúunii   inguust   hánsanaan
and then   chaats chuunii   across from   too
tlagaay   tl'   kyaadáayaan
land   they   went

And then they moved to across from Chaats Chuunii too.

tl'áa	an	nang	útl'aakdaas	tl'áa	an	nang k'ajáas
them	for	the	chief	them	for	the leader

tlak	l	kwatáalang	tlaa	gam	Gan	dii	wunsitang
what	he	died	that	not	what	I	know don't

gin	st'	l	kwatáalang	tlaa[33]
thing	from	he	died	that

Their chief, their leader, the reason he died, I don't know what he died of.

l	kwatáhls	gyaenuu	tl'	na'áans	ingúust
he	died	and		they living	across from

Gantl	xujúu	kwayáans
water	small	flowing

tlagáay	laas	q'átsgát	laa	esgáay	guu
land	nice	beautiful	good	there	is where

nang	útl'aakdaas	tl'	hlGáeuuwaayaan
the	chief		they buried

He died, and they were living across from Small-water-that-flows, good ground, beautiful scenery; it was there they buried the man.

lei	a	hluu	esgáays	gántl	kwa	xujúus	ki 'aas	kyaanaan
him	for	is what	there	water	small	flowing	named	but

gam	ki 'u	an	dii	wúnsitanggan
not	name	self	I	know don't

It is for him they named (a) small flowing creek but I don't know the name.

waa saliiaa o	chíinaa	tl'	aa	Gilgats	dluu
after that	fish	they	theirs	dry	when

tlakw	tl'	qayáan	aa	tl'	ch'áak	xajáawaan
what	they	found	to	they	move	all

After that (since then), when they dry their fish they all move to the place they found.

esgáay	kasáan	iijing
there	Kasaan	is

It is Kasaan.

wed	old kasáan	hínuu	tl'	kyáat
now	Old Kasaan	is what	they	call (it)

Now they call it "Old Kasaan."

---

[33] *tlak*, "reason"; *tlaa*, "what he died of"

íkwaan uu   esgáay   xaatáay   kasáan   aa   ga-ch'aagáayaan
but   then   people   Kasaan   to   moved
But it was then people moved to Kasaan.

xaatáay uu   yáadaas xaatáay uu   ijáan
people   yaadaas Haida   were
The people were the Yaadaas Haida clan.

gyaagan   xaatgáay uu   yáadaas   íijing
my   people   yaadaas   are
My people are Yaadaas.

esgáayst duu   gam   tlíisdluu   esgáayst
from then   not   when   from there
new kasáan   aa   tl'   ch'aagáayaan
New Kasaan   to   they   moved
tlaa   gam   Gan   dii   wúnsitaanggan
that   not   that   I   don't know
From there they moved to New Kasaan but I don't know (when).

gin haganáan   dlang   hl   díiaan   suudaas   aehluu
reason   you   I   really   tell   with
yáadaas xaatáayk   wáajaagantgaangaan
yaadaas Haida   struggled
The reason I'm really telling you this is because the Yaadaas people really struggled.

q'wíitaas xaatáay   ch'aagáayaan   dluu
muddy-mouth people   moved   when
q'índats   daals   dluu   tl'   iijaan
summer   near   when   they   did
The muddy-mouth people moved when it was near summer.

ahljíihluu   tláa   an   gin   láagaangaan
for this reason   them   for   things   good were
For this reason things were good for them.

íkwaan   yáadaas xaatáay   tla-ch'aagáayaan
but   yaadaas people   moved
dluu   cháanuut   geíisdluu
when   fall   becoming
But when the Yaadaas people moved it was becoming fall.

xaataay   ch'aagáay   dluu   tlii   tlaak   wáajaagantgaangaan
yaadaas   moved   when   much   for them   struggle
When the Yaadaas people moved it was such a struggle for them.

singaays   tlíi   daGangáas   gyaen   tadáas
weather   so much bad   and   cold
íkwaan   gin haganáan   dlank   Gahl   hl   gyaehlándaas   dluu
but   reason   to you   it   I   told   when
yáahl   tláa   qagándaayaan
raven   them   saved

**The weather was so bad and cold but that's the reason I told you
about when Raven saved them.**

yáahl   tláa   qagándaayaan   hluu
raven   them   saved   is where
tlak   aehl   is   tl'   tláagaangaan   kyaatdáayaan   ch'aats chuunii
place   at   is   they   first   called   chaats chuunii

**The Raven saved them at that place they first called Chaats
Chuunii.**

xaat   kil   tl'   gyaehlándaas   gam   díian   tlíijii   dánuu
Haida language they story-tell   not   really anywhere while

**When we (they) tell stories in Haida (they're) not really just
anywhere.**

áa   tlang   kil   kwánjuu   daalgang   gyaehlingaay
it   we   talk anywhere going along story-telling

Our talk goes anywhere storytelling.

uugyaen   yáalaay   haganáan   yáadaas   chaagáay   laagáalaan
and then   raven   because   yaadaas   place   nice became

**And then because of the Raven, the Raven people's living conditions
got nice.**

hayáan uu   yaats xaatáay   gin   suutgans   dlangk   hl   suudaasaan
still   white people   thing say   to you   I   say will
gam   gat   tl'   q'iisgatan   isgyaen   tl'   appreciate-gíigan
not   it   they forget   and   they appreciate always

**They still too—(as) white people say I will say to you folks—they
didn't forget it and then too they always appreciate.**

kasáan   tlagáay   láagaan
Kasaan   land   nice

Kasaan land was nice.

chíinaays   waa   kwáan
fish   there plentiful

Fish were plentiful.

qáadaays   waak   duungáa
deer   there   near
Deer were near there.

Carta Bay   aehl   sanáan   sGwáaganaay
Carta Bay   at   too   sockeye

duungáas   gyaen   kwaan
near   and   many
At Carta Bay too, sockeye were near and plentiful.

an   tl'   xas   laagaan   yáadaas xaatáay
selves they   move about   good   Yaadaas Haida
They made a good move, the Yaadaas people.

qwítaas xaatáay   hansanaan   ch'aagáay   laagáalaan
muddy-mouth people   too   situation   nice became
The muddy-mouth people too, their welfare got nice.

gyaehlingaay   kwáanang
stories   much not
The story wasn't much.

íkwaan   tlíijiidaan   Gántl   kwaayáans uu
but   much-starting water   flowing

tl'   qayáa uu   tláagaanaan
they   found   first

hluu   wed   esgáay   xaatáay   gyaao   is
when   now   there   people   's   is

an   tl'ang   súugank   xitáa uu
self   we   say   Hedda Creek
But the place, where they first found water running, now that place is theirs; we say Hedda Creek.

q'wii xaatáay gyaa uu   Gandlaay   iijing
muddy-mouth people's   water   is
It's the muddy-mouth people's water.

iik   Gándlaay   hansanáan   q'wii xaatáas gyaa   iijing
it   water   too   muddy-mouth people's   is
The creek too is the muddy-mouth people's.

íkwaan   st   chíin   tl'   istaas   gam   xaa   tl'   saao is hlgangang
but   from fish   they   take   not   people they   resent
But if they (others) get fish from there the people don't resent it.

q'wii xaatáas   Gahl   aa   q'áng-gwudang
muddy-mouth people it   with be generous
The muddy-mouth people are (always) generous with their (creek).

gam   tl'   kil   guusúuwaagank
not   they   word   argue
They don't bicker about it.

tlíisdluu   gut   stihláas   dluu   tl'   ístgank
much   each   want   when   they   take
They take as much as they want.

áao   tlaan   gyaehlingaay   díingaay   Giidang   Giitl
it   no more   story   my   condition   is finished
My story is finished.

A Skidegate Raid on the Bella Coola

Ninstints	*xaatáay*	*Kaisun*	*aa*	*tluu*	*stánsang*	*gwaa*
Ninstints	people	Kaisun	to	canoes	four	on

Gaayhldáa	*aan uu*	*gut*	*tlíi*	*ginángk*	*íntlaa'aayaan*
fighting	for	together	to help	ask	came

The Ninstints people came to Kaisun in four canoes to ask the people to go to war with them.[34]

uugyaen	*Ninstints*	*xaatáay*	*sanaan*	*tlúu*
and then	Ninstints	people	too	

stánsang	*gwaa*	*tl'aehl*	*ijáan*
canoes	four	on	them with were

Then they went along in four canoes.

tláanaayk	*ingúust*	*tl'*	*Gús*	*dluu*
mainland	across	they	were	when

Bentinck	*xáaw*	*iik*	*xwu-isjáayaan*
Bentinck	Arm	into	sail-into

After they had crossed (to the mainland), they entered Bentinck Arm.

gyáak	*tl'*	*Gaayhldáas*	*ingúust uu*	*Gaalgáa*	*staahl*	*tl'*	*Gasgadáan*
where	they	fighting	across	while	dark	they	landed

And they went in opposite the fort during the night.

uugyaen	*guu*	*ga*	*náangaan*	*t'úts*	*tláa*	*tsánhluu-iidaan*
and then	there	they	living	some	them	shooting start

Then some people who had been camping in the inlet began firing from in front.

esgáay guu	*Amai'kuns*	*tl'*	*tiiáayaan*
at that place	Amai'kuns	they	killed

There Amai'kuns was killed.

giitlagún	*hánsanaan*	*tl'*	*tla-gáaydaayaan*
Floating	too	they	wounded

They also wounded Floating.

---

[34] The English text here appears essentially as Swanton presented it (Swanton 1911:281-82). The story is hard to follow in places, especially when it is not clear who "they," "he," and "we" are.

"The Ninstints people came to Kaisun in four canoes to ask the people to go to war with them."

kwiiáas	hánsanaan	chagáan	láak	tl'	tla-gáaydaayaan
Beloved	too	shot	him	they	wounded

They shot and wounded Beloved too.

tláa	suu duu	gudingáay	tláatsgáa	jahlíigaan
people	among	mind	strong	most was

He was a brave man among them.

uugyaan	tl'	xaataas	stáng uu	Xáldang	aan	tl'	istáayaan
and then	they	people	two	slave	for	they	took

There they also enslaved two persons.

waasalíaa oo	haósanaan	sta	tl'	xwu-istiidaan
after that	once again	from	they	sail-start

After that they started out.

sti	guu	ist	xwu-istii	tláagaans	t'úts uu
from	there	leaving	sail-leave	first	some
haósanaan	ga	xwu-istáalgaays	tl'	qingáenaan
once again	those	sail-coming	they	see-went to

And those who started first went out to some people who were coming along under sail.

jakw	xwastáng	tl'	jántluus uu	guu	tl'	gudáangaan
guns	two	they	shooting	there	they	heard

The noise of two guns was heard.

wasalíaa oo	tluuwáay	q'áaluu	gii-Gaaydáng
afterwards	canoe	empty	float-empty did
uugyaen	tl'	jaadáa	stáng uu	Xáldaang	aan	tl'	istáayaan
and then	they	women	two	slave	for	they	took

Afterwards the canoe drifted away empty, and they enslaved two women.

t'úts   hánsanaan   tl'aa   gwii   gúu   ii   iijáan
some   too   them   to   there   to   were
láanaayk   aa   náan   aa uu   tl'   gút   tl'   tlagáangaan
land   at   close   to   they   float   they   more than one
guut   xaataa   gitsgiitdáayaan   Gahl   tl'   gudingáay   laa aa
there   people   captured   with them   they   mind   happy
tl'   xaatáas   k'álat   hánsanaan   kuń   xadúu
they   people   different   too   point   around
tlúu   gwaa   xwu-k'áagaan   tláa   tl'   qíns   gyaen uu   tluuwáa-st
canoes   on   sail-came   them   they   saw   and   canoes from
an   tl'   ta-gudáang   taelaan
selves   they   jump   motion from edge down

**(The others) came thither, and while they lay close to the land,
rejoicing over the persons captured, some people came sailing
around a point in a canoe, saw them and jumped off.**

án   tlaa   tagudáangaan   esgáayst   án
those   they   jumped   afterwards   those
gugya'áayaan   t'lang   xidii'   údaan
ran away   we   chased

Then we landed in pursuit of them.

ámjuwaan uu   án   hl   tla-Gúhl   gwadáng
for a little while   self   I   get ready   tried
án   hl   tla-Gúhldaas   dluu   hláa'aa   sanaan   sta   katéilgan
self   I   finished   when   me   too   from   got off

And after I had spent some little time preparing myself, I got off.

Gándlaay   gúut   nang   án   gyaat   dliiáandaas uu   hl   xidii'údaan
water   along   one   self   fleeing   running   I   chased

**And I started to pursue one person who was running about near the
sea.**

dútsii   qáahlii   laa   hl   xiijiiláang   kaóduu
woods in   inside   him   I   chased   a while
Gándlaay   ii   án   l   gyaa   Gáatguugan
water   into   self   he   fled   jumping

**After I had chased him about in the woods for a while, he jumped
into the ocean.**

l   qáts   aehluu   láa   hl   gítsgats   dluu   gíntajaay   laa   hl   istgán
his   hair   with   him   I   holding onto   when   blanket   his   I   took

**And I took his hair, along with his (yellow-cedar bark) blanket,
away from him.**

Gándlaayst   a gwódang aan   l   dlak tl'aahlgán   gyaen
water from   he   swim to me   and
stláangs   saa   dii   Xánts guu duu   l   kayínslaas   dii   l   qíndatgan
hands   up   my face   he giving up   me   he showed
**And he came up out at sea and held up his hands in front of my face
(in token of surrender).**

esgáayst uu   táajaay   gwii   dii   gwíi   l   dlakgan
and then afterward   beach   to   me   toward he swam
Then he swam shoreward toward me.

díi   an   l   dáng-eigan   uugyaan   haós   Gándlaay   ii
me to self he close came   and then   once again water   into
l   Gáatgan   gyaen   q'atgwáao   án   dii   l   qíndatgan
he jumped   and   out a little ways self me   he showed
wáadluu   laa   hl   jántluu-iidaan
and then as a result him   I   shooting at started
**When he got near me he dove again and came to the surface out at
sea, and I began to shoot at him.**

láangaay   gwíi   haós   l   dlakgán   gyaen   tlaalingáay
the land   towards once again he swam   and   the cliff
dawúl guu duu   án   l   sGélgat   án   dukw   dla-t'íijan
side   self he hiding   self against body-did hold
**Then he swam landward and held himself tightly against the face of
a certain cliff.**

láa   hl   jas   stáns   dluu   tláan   hl   wáagan
him   I   shot twice   when no more   I   did
After I had shot at him twice there, I stopped.

esgáayst uu   qíit   tlaalingáay   gya'áang   ís
and then afterwards   tree cliff   standing   is
gwíiuu   ang   l   qagándatgan
onto   self he saved
Then he climbed up upon a tree standing upon the face of the cliff.

qíidaay   sáasii   qátgwaa   tlaalingáayst   ist gyáenaan uu   gwíi   an
tree   top   out   cliff from was   even if   towards self
l   dukw-Xiid   ámtsuuwaan   Gíhl   dluu   tlaalingáay   l   gitsgíhlt
he struggle did after while   became when cliff   he catch
**And although its top was some distance from the cliff, he bent it
toward it, and after a while got hold of the face of the cliff.**

tlaalingáay	*xúlaas*	*ii guu*	*l*	*án*	*dla-dlhl*
cliff	hole	into	he	self	body-whole

And he went into a hole in it.

gám tlak	*Xitgáang*	*isgyaen*	*sagwúst*
no way	down	or	up from

l	*Gú-tlingei*	*aa*	*l*	*qáengaa-anggaan*
he	become could	it	he	find not

He could not go from it either downward or upward.

hín uu	*gut*	*ga*	*t'láng*	*súugiinii*
this is what	each other	it	we	said to

Gáa	*l*	*gutáalaansaang*	*xúlaas aa*
inside	he	die will	hole in

We said to one another that he would die right in it.

wáadlaa uu	*esgáayst*	*tluuwáay*	*gwaa*	*sta*	*tl'*	*ist údaan*
afterwards	after	canoes	on	from	they	started

After (they could see there's no escape for him), then they started from that place in their canoes.

uugyaen	*tl'*	*ch'áanuugan*	*gyaen*	*gut*	*gutáao*	*tl'*	*istgan*
and then	they	fire did	and	each other	food	they	gave

Then they had a fire and began to give each other food.

waasalíaa	*haósanaan*	*sta*	*tl'*	*istúd*	*esgáaysduu*	*haósanaan*
after all this	once again	from	they	leave started	and then	once again

guu	*tl'*	*Gaayhltdáas*	*xaatáay*	*aan*	*tl'*	*Gaayhltdii'údaan*
there	they	fighting	people	at	they	fight start

And after they again started off, they again began fighting with the fort.

wáadluu	*gám tlakw*	*án*	*qagándaa*	*hlingéi*	*qáenggaan*	*guu*
and then	no way	self	save	could	find	

hútl'	*xiditlaagán*
there we	arrived

Then we got into a position from which we could not get away.

gam tlak	*án*	*qagándaa*	*hlingéi*	*qáenggaa'ang*
no way	self	save	could	find not

Gúdandaanuu	*tlúugwaay*	*hútl'*	*tl'*	*qagánt*	*íntlaagan*
while	canoes on	us	they	to save	arrived

Then, although we could not get away at first, they finally got us into (the canoes).

"And after they had lain out to sea for some time, a man wearing a dancing blanket and cedar bark rings dragged down a canoe and came out to us, accompanied by a woman."

uugyaen   nang   sGwáansang uu[35]   *náay   úngwii   án   l   tluuhláayaan*
and then   one   one   house   on top   self   he   climbed up
And a certain person crept around on top of the house.

láa   tl'   chagán   gyaen uu   l   dlawúteilgaan
him   they   shot   and   he   body-fell-down-did
They shot him so that he fell down.

Gandlaayk   gíi-tlagán   kaóduu   nang   úhlingaa   xyáahl   gíntas
water   float-motionless   a while   one   man   dance   blanket
isgyaen   stliihluu   gy'aenándaayaan uu   thíu   Gandlaay   ii   dáng
and   rings   wearing   canoe   water   into   pulled
k'úhleslaayaan   híitl   aa   l   tlúu-qáatlaagan
motion did   us   to   he   rowed to
nang   jáada   leihl   íijan
one   woman   him with   was
And after they had lain out to sea for some time, a man wearing a
dancing-blanket and cedar-bark rings dragged down a canoe and
came out to us, accompanied by a woman.

Tldóogwaang   gyaa   tluuwáay   gyaa   tl'
Tldoogwaang   's   canoe   on   they
iijáan uu   láa   aa   tl'   gúusuu'aawaan
were   him   to   they   talked
And those in Tldoogwaang's canoe talked to them.

nang   jáadaas   an   Gahl gwíuu   tláak   gwíuu
the   woman   to   closer   them to   toward
láa   an   tl'   hlGei'áayaan   nang   úhlingaas   tl'   tiiáa'asaan
her   to   they   asked   the   man   they   kill would
tl'   sáawaan   wáadluu   Gándlaay   ii   l   dlawíigaasaan
they   said   and then   water   into   he   body-fall would
Then they told the woman to come closer, and said that they should
shoot the man so that he would fall into the water.

Tldóogwaang   ga   gwáawaayaan   uugyaen   tláa   sta   tluu-qáayd-iidaan
Tldoogwaang   it   refused   and then   them   from   row-go-started
Tldoogwaang refused and started away from them.

wáagyaen   sta   án   tl'   gyaa'áayaan
and then   from   self   they   fled
Then they fled away in terror.

---

[35] *nang* = a, one (person); *sGwáansang* = one, a (number)

jakwgaay   tláa   Gíilaawaan
shells   theirs   all gone were
Their ammunition was all gone.

t'láng   hánsanaan   waasalíiaa   sta   áng   gyaa-iidaan
we   too   afterward   from   selves   flee started
Then we also started off.

uugyaen   djíidaao   kúnst uu   xwu-istii-íidaan
and then   Djiidaao   Point   sail from started
Gáhl   stánsangs   Gándlaay guu   l   gíitlagaang   kaóduu
night   four   water   they float   a while
Cape St. James   aehl   l   ístlaa'uugan
Cape St. James   to   they   came
**Then they started from Point Djiidaao, and after they had spent
four nights upon the sea, they came to Cape St. James.**

Gáhl   stáng   l   xwu-qáa uu   kaóduu
night   two   they   sail-go   a while
Kaisun   aehl   l   Giditlaa'uugan
Kaisun   at   they   arrived
After they had traveled two more nights, they came to Kaisun.

ginhl   táan áan an   tla-Gíihldaa   kyáanaanuu
what they started to do,   went after by boat   made finished   instead of
sihlgaan   tl'   Giditláa   gám   aa   tl'   tla- Gíidaan
back   they   arrived   not   it   they   finished
tlak   jíingaas duu   gínggaangaan uu   sihlgáang   l   Gititláa'uugan
country   far   for nothing   back   they   arrived
**Instead of accomplishing what they had hoped, they returned from
a far country almost emptyhanded.**

áao   tláan   gyaehlingáay   díingaa   Gíidan
here   no more   story   mine   is
Here this story comes to an end.

First Kill

awáahl Gagwíɪ nang íıhlingaa xuujúu gin   tíɪ
a long time   ago   person   small   something killed
tláagaans dluu Gan laa tl'   yakwdánggaangaan
first   when it   him they honored

**A long time ago when a boy child first killed something, they
honored him for it.**

tlak gin   Xíɪningaa hánuu saa   Gan laa tl'   gudángaangaan
any   thing alive   any   high it   him they thought

For any living thing, they thought highly of him for it.

gin   hán   aa   k'áat sdlúk Xuut saa   Gan laa tl'
thing any   for deer   mink   seal high it   his they
gudán   stist   dan   hl   laa tl'   láaganganggaangaan
thought because event with him they celebrated

**For any thing—deer, mink, seal—because they thought so highly of
it, they celebrated it with him.**

tl'   wáadluaan guu tl'   dúugaangan
them all   they invited

They invited everyone.

l   íɪtlaagudáa gaasdluu uwáa t'álguu
he of means   if was   much more
saa   Gan laa tl'   gwadánggaangaan
high it   his they thought

**If he was high on the totem pole, that much more highly of him
they thought for it.**

san Gisgyaan
day what kind of
laa xadúu   ga   na   háangsgaay   ga   tl'   dúusgyaan
him around those living around there   those they invited

**Depending on the occasion, those living around him were the ones
they invited.**

táawaays wáa an   laa tl'   Gíɪhlgaangan Gíihlt
food   it   for his they prepared finished

They prepared a lot of food for his celebration.

wáahlahl dlúu uu   Gan laa tl'   gudánggaangaan
potlatch as much as it   his they thought

They thought as much of his event as of a potlatch.

tl'	*xyáahl*	*kaóduu*	*taawaay*	*is*	*Gúhl*	*giisdluu*
they	dance	a while	food	there	prepared	when

tl'	*hldanúu-iidaangaan*
they	feast started

After dancing quite a while, when the food was all prepared they started to eat.

saa	*tl'*	*gudángaay*	*q'iin*	*aóduu*	*wáa*	*an*	*Giditláas*	*dluu*
over	they	minds	warm	after while	it	for	time	when

nang	*úhlingaa*	*xuujúus*	*gyaa*	*gin*	*tiiáayaan*
the	small	boy	of	thing	killed

ga hl	*laa*	*tl'*	*kuyánggaangaan*
it with	his	they	show off

After their minds feel warm over the food for so long, the time for it arrives; the thing the small boy killed, they show off with it.

asgáay uu	*hinuu*	*Gan*	*laa*	*tl'*	*gudáangaan*
that is	the way	it	his	they	honored

That is the way they honored his deed.

laa	*tl'*	*singáada*
him	they	day give

They give him the day.

hínuu	*tl'*	*kyaatganggan*
this way	they	call

That is what they call it.

Mother's Brother's First Kill

dii   aao   daa   tsúujuus dluu
my   mother's   brother   small   when
xitút xuujúu   "bow n arrow"   hl   l   tiiáayaan
bird   small   bow 'n' arrow   with   he   killed
**When my mother's brother was small he killed a small bird with a
bow and arrow.**

wáadluu xaatgáay gwu   náans Gan   aan uu gu   tl'   dáawaan
then   people   there living those to   them they invited
Just the people living there at that time were the ones they invited.

tl'   xyaahls gaayst tl'   hldanúu Gúhldaas dluu
they   dance   after   they   eat   finished   when
tsaatsgáay   ts'ahl   ungkw laa tl'   xatlaasáayaan
bird   pillow   on   his   they brought out
Gan laa   tl'   gudán   stist
it   good   they thought because
**After they danced and when they finished eating, they brought out
his little bird on a pillow because they thought it was so cute.**

hawún   sanaan tl'   xyáahl-iidaan
once   again   they dance start
Once again they started dancing.

xúutlakw dii   aao   diik   gyaahlántgan
the way   my   mother   me to   told
That's the way my mother told me the story.

The Scaredest I've Ever Been in My Life

awaahl	*tl' ínats*	*dluu*	*Copper Mt.*	*aa*	*tl'*	*ch'aak*	*xuujúugiinii*
long ago	summer	when	Copper Mt.	to	they	move	all used to

tl'	*aadéit*	*kunáast*	*'families'gaay*	*guut*	*eihl*	*skáadang*	*íngiinii*
they	seine	before	families	together	with	berrypick	used to

Long ago, when they used to seine at Copper Mountain, families used to berry pick together.

"cannery"gaay	*ingúust*	*duu*	*Gantl*	*Gawyáanggan*
cannery	across	from	creek	bay was

There was a creek across the bay from the cannery.

wáa	*t'áay*	*guu*	*skóanaay*	*kwáangiinii*
at	the mouth	is where	berries	many used to be

There used to be a lot of berries at the mouth of the creek.

Copper Mt.	*ehluu*	*táan*	*kwáangiinii*
Copper Mt.	at	bears	many used to be

There used to be a lot of bears at Copper Mountain.

inguust	*Gandlaay*	*aa*	*ii*	*istáalgan-gíɰgiinii*
across	the creek	at	to	go used to

aak	*tlii*	*dii*	*aoláng*	*Gaanaayk*	*stahlgáangaahl*
there to	much	my	parents	went back

My parents used to go there often.

tl'	*aadiidEít*	*kunáast*	*ingwii*	*tl'ang*	*skáadang*	*íngan*
they	fish start	before	across	we	berrypick	went

Before they started fishing we went berry picking.

sin	*Giduu*	*sanaan*	*l*	*hlkwiit*	*waan*	*hlGáandanggan*
what	reason	too	they	hurried	were	I thought

I thought they were hurrying for some reason.

waadluu	*hayáan*	*dii*	*Gaa*	*xuujúugan*
and then	still	I	child	small was

ikwaan	*dii*	*skáadaang*	*Gáayaagiinii*
but	I	berrypick	good used to be

And then I was still a small child but I used to be a good berry picker.

Gaa   tl'ang   skáadaang   íngan   dluu   sín   yeihl   an   Gáandanggan
there we   berrypick   went   when   what evening to   getting was
hlGayk'yúust   uu   tl'ang   skáadaang
in a hurry   is how   we   picked berries
**When we went there berry picking and it was getting close to
evening, we picked berries in a hurry!**

táanaay   kwáadangaay   wáa   Gadúu   kwaan
bear   droppings   there around   many
There were many bear droppings around there.

yánggyaen uu   an   hl   gwahl   xwáagangsgwaanuu
really,   self me   death   scared really
Really, I was scared to death!

klakwáanan uu   hl   hlGayk'yúust   skáadaans-gwaan
any old way is how   I   in a hurry   berrypicked really
I was picking berries just any old way.

yanggyaen uu   an   dii   hlxuuhl   gwatalsaan   hl   Gaandanggan
really   self I   fright   die would   I   felt
I really thought I would die of fright!

húu tlis núut tlíi   dii   hlxwáalgaayaan   hl   gudáng
much   I   frightened   I   think
táanaayk   án   hl   xugwatalsgan
bears   self I   die
I was so frightened of the bears I thought I'd die.

Gáa   hl   gudáng-gígan
about this   I   think used to
I used to think about my experience.

gam   aoláng   eihl   kyáananganggan
not   parents   to I   call (ask) didn't
uugyaens   gam   láak   hl   súutaanuugan   tlii   dii   hlxwáagan
and   not   them   I   told them   much   I   scared was
I never asked my parents about it or told them how scared I was.

esgáayst   hánuu   táan   dii   ga-hlxwaak   gii
after that   any   bears   I   scared   used to be
After that I used to be scared of any bears.

tlak	*sihlgáang*	*'cannery'gaay*	*aa*	*tl'ang*	*ijáan*	*tl'aa aa*
how	back	cannery	to	we	went	really

gam	*da*	*díi*	*gujúuang*
not	it	I	remember don't

How we got back to the cannery, I don't remember.

gam	*dii*	*Xíinangaa aang waas*	*dluu*
not	I	living	when

gam	*wed*	*Gahl*	*dlangk*	*gyaehlándaa*	*hlingáa'anggan*
not	now	about it	you to	storytell	couldn't

But if I didn't live through it, I couldn't be telling you about it now.

aao	*tlaan*	*gyaehlingaay*	*diingaa*	*Gíidang*
here	no more	story	mine	isn't

There's no more to my story.

ha'waa
thank you
Thank you.

Paul's Name

díi   gít   Paul aa   áastluu   l   stúujuus dluu   áastluu   l   kwáay
my   son   Paul   this much he   small   when   this much his   hips
láa   Gáanggaas   gyaenaan   l   q'ulúu   áastluu   laa   dliladaa
his   big   but   his   legs   this much his   big around
**When my son Paul was *this* small, his hips were *this* big, but his legs
were _this_ big around.**

l   Gáay   aa   kwajúu   óyaagan
he   fat   short   very much
He was very short and fat.

wáadluu   Puujii   Gáang aa   uu
and then   Puujii   and them
skúul   naayst   istla'aas   dluu   Gáagaay   láa   an   qíntaagúnii
school   house   from came   when   children   him   to   look at used to
**And then Puujii and them, when they came from the schoolhouse,
the children used to look at him.**

waadluu   "kwáay íiwaans"   hín   láa   tl'ang kyaagúigan gwaa
at that time   "big butt"   this is him   we   name did   truly
At that time "Big Butt" is the name we gave him.

wáagyaen uu   Mrs Davis   awáa   k'wahl q'awáas   dluu
and then   Mrs. Davis mother by   sitting   when
hingáan   Gahl   laa   tl'ang   kil   náangs dluu uu
in jest   with it   the name we   language play   when
**And then when Mrs. Davis was visiting mother, we were just
making fun calling him "Big Butt."**

húu   kyaa   láa   láa   újing
that   name   high class his   is
láak   láa   hl   isdáang   hínuu   Mrs Davis   suu
to him the name I   give   this   Mrs. Davis says
**"That name of his is high class; I give him the name," is what Mrs.
Davis said.**

kyaa   íiwaan uu   újing   "kwáay íiwaans"
name   big   is   is   kwaay iiwaans
"It's a big name, 'kwaay iiwaans.' "

'kwáhgáay íiwaans'   hínuu   tl'   súudaang
'kwaahgaay iiwaans'   this   they   pronounce
" 'Kwahgaay iiwaans' is the way you pronounce it."

wáadluu   gam   hútl'   gyaa   'clan'gaay   namegaay   is
and so   not   us   's   clan   name   is
ans   gyaenaan uu   Mrs Davis uu   láak   láa   istgan
ours   but   Mrs. Davis   to him   it   gave
And so it's not our clan name, but Mrs. Davis gave it to him.

ahljú   yáh   kyaa   an   l   súus   dluu   láak   láa   l   istgan
truly   true   name   self   she   said   when   to him   it   she   gave
"It's really a true name," she said, when she gave it to him.

l   ki'úuu   kwáay úwaans   hin   laa   Gúdang
his   name   *kwáay úwaans*   this   his   is
"This is his name, *'kwaay iiwaans.'* "

Psalm 46: God Is with Us

sáan   iitl'aakdaas uu   hiitl'   ga stáng[36]
high   chief   us   two

God is with us.

sáan   iitl'aakdaas   aehluu   hiitl'   qaganáa
high   chief   with   we   saved

With him we are saved. (God is our shelter and our strength.)

tl'áa-k   tlaadéian   l   Giihlgiigaa   gíigan
to them   to help   He   ready   all the time

Always ready to help (in times of trouble).

waadluu   gam   híitl'   hlxwaakaansaan
so   not   we   afraid will be

So we will not be afraid.

tlagáay   yildang   dawáanuu   uugyaen   tlat'awáay   sanáan
earth   shaken   even if   and   the mountains   too
ch'a'áan   hldii'iingáas   gii   ch'ahl   dawáanuu   gam   hiitl'   hlxwáakansaan
ocean   depths   into   fall   even if   not   we   afraid will be

Even if the earth is shaken and the mountains too, even if they fall into the ocean depths, we will not be afraid.

klíisdluu   "seas"gaay   xáluudaa   dawáanuu   uugyaen   "seas"gaay
no matter how much   the seas   action of   even if   and   the seas
gin   káahliihlt   gans gingaan   gudingaa   dawáanuu   uugyaen
things   into a rage   like   sound   even if   and
k'wajuuwáas   yíldang   dawáanuu   hayaanuu   gam   hiitl'   hlxwaakansaan
the hills   shaking   even if   even then   not   we   afraid will be

No matter how much the seas roll and how much the seas (throw) things into a rage like the sound of the hills shaking, even then we will not be afraid.

---

[36] *hiitl'aehl stáng* = make us two in one.

Gantl iiwaan kwayaans uu gudingaay laa uu
water big flows mind happy
sáan iitl'aakdaas gwii isdáa'asaan
high chief to brings
sáan iitl'aakdaas gyaa naay kwii'áas hansanaan
high chief 's house sacred too
gudingaay laa l istáa'asaan
mind happy it brings
There is a river that brings joy to God and to God's sacred house.

esgaay tlagaay guu saan iitl'aakdaas iijing
in that city God is
God is in that city.

gam gin haganáanuu
not thing happens
tlagáay laa hláanstliiaa hlingáa ang gan
city his destroyed could not be
No matter what happens his city could not be destroyed.

singaay Gatgéihls dluu Gándlaayk l tláa'atsaan
early at dawn is when river he help will
gwaay kingaas hlxwáakasaan saa tlagaay hansanaan yíldang
the earth terrified will be high land too are shaken
In the early dawn he'll help the river, the earth will be terrified,
kingdoms too are shaken.

sáan iitl'akdaas húlangs sGi qajaang
God roaring red blasting
uugyaen tlagaay sanaan hldamíits[37]
and the earth too dissolves
God, roaring, blasting red (God thunders) and the earth goes up in
flames.

sáan iitl'aakdaas an yakdángaas uu hiitl' aehl stánggang
God self almighty is us with two are
God's mighty self is one with us.

Jacob Xáat hluu hiitl' qaganáagan
Jacob's father with us safety is
We are safe with Jacob's father.

---

[37] *hldamíits* = "dissolved, burnt in a quick fire"; *hldáamit* = "ashes."

hahlgwáa-kwaa   tlakw   sáan iitl'akdaas   gin   tla-Gíihldaayaan   qing
come see   what   God   thing has done   soo
Come, see what God has done!

kwáa   tlíi   gin   q'aldingáa   Giit
what   bunch things amazing   down
tlagáay   gin   l   tla-Gíihldaayaan
earth   things he   finished
What amazing things he finished on earth!

q'iiduu   hlingwáa   tlagáay q'as gwa'áan guu   l   tla-Gíihl   daal
wars   the earth   the whole land   he stops   all over
He stops wars all over the land.

hlGiit   l   tla-Gánggaas   kitáao   sanaan   l   hl'aanshl
bows   he   snaps   spears   too   he destroys
He snaps bows and destroys spears.

uugyaen   t'a'áao   sanaan   l   Gúdit
and   shields   too   he lets burn up
He lets shields burn up.

tláanhl   Gáayhl duu   hínuu   suu
stop   fighting   this is what he said
"Stop fighting!" is what he said.

íkwaan   hl   díuu   sáan iitl'aakdaas   an
but   I   myself God   himself
an tl'   únsitgídaang   gwáayk   aan   sáa uu   díi   q'uláa
ourselves know all the time   nations   to   above   I   supreme
hlinggwáay   tlagáays   sáa   díi   q'ulaa
the world   too   above   I   supreme
**But I myself, God himself, we ourselves know all the time he is
supreme above nations, supreme above the world.**

sáan iitl'aakdaas   kwiiáas   híitl'   aehl   stánggang
God   almighty us   with   two in one
God almighty is one with us.

Jacob   Xáat uu   aehl uu   hiitl'   qaganáagang
Jacob's father   with   us   saves
Jacob's father saves us.

aao   tlaan   gyaehlingaay   Giidang
this no more   scriptures   are
This is the end of the scripture.

ha'waa,   *ha'waa*
thank you,   thank you
Thank you. Thank you.

dlang   an   hl   kil laagan
you   self   I   thank
I thank you.

ha'waa
thank you
Thank you.

sáan iitl'aakdaas   híitl'   aehl   stánggei   Gans guu   dii   gudánggang
God   us   with   twice   like   I   hope, pray
I pray that the Lord will bless us twofold.

ha'waa
thank you
Thank you.

How to Make Fried Bread

sablii	*dang*	*tlaautlaas*	*dluu*
bread	you	make	when

When you are going to make bread

sabliigaay	*waa'aan aa*	*tl'*	*kwiidang*
flour	it for	they	measure

you measure your flour for it.

Gantl	*isgyaen*	*tang*	*isgyaen*	*suugaa*
water	and	salt	and	sugar

Water and salt and sugar

guutsuuwiit	*tl'*	*skanguulaan*
together	they	stir together

they stir together.

aa	*tl'*	*k'iinsdaan*	*'milk'*
it	they	warm	milk

You warm the milk.

Gantl	*skatlaangwei*	*tlehl*	*dluu*	*aa*	*tl'*	*kwiidang*
water	cups	5	when	it	they	measure

You measure about 5 cups of water,

suugaagaay	*hans*	*sdlaagwaa*	*sdángsaan*	*dluu*	*wei aa*	*tl'*	*kwiidang*
sugar	too	spoons	2	when	about	they	measure

about 2 spoons of sugar, too.

tang	*sdlaagwaa*	*tsuujuu*	*hlGúnahl*	*wei aa*	*tl'*	*kwiidang*
salt	spoons	little	3	about	they	measure

Three teaspoons of salt,

taao	*sdlaagwaal*	*iiwaan*	*xwastáng*	*wei aa*	*tl'*	*kwiidang*
oil	spoons	big	2	about	they	measure

2 big spoonfuls of oil,

aajii	*kaahlaawaay*	*hans*	*hlGúnahl*	*dluu*
and then	yeast	too	3	when

about 3 cakes of yeast,

Gantl	*ii*	*sga-sGwáansang*	*ii uu*	*laagan*
water	in	one (cup)	in	is good

into about a cup of water is fine.

aajii	*sabliigaay*	*ii*	*suuga*	*tang*	*taaoaay*
and then	the bread	into	sugar	salt	oil

(Put) sugar, salt, oil into this bread.

aajii	*waadluaan*	*guutsuuwiit*	*gaa*	*dang*	*skanjuulaan*
and then	all	together	it	you	stir

Stir this whole thing together.

asgaayst	*dang*	*skwokaatsaa'aasaang*
and then	you	knead

And then you knead.

asgaayst	*taao*	*guut*	*dang*	*gaanaansaang*
and then	oil	on it	you	rub

And then you rub oil on it.

asgaayst	*k'uusk'iit*	*sGwáansaang*	*dang*	*kaahl-daa'aasaan*
and then	rise	once	you	rise make do

And then let it rise once.

aajii	*kaahl-daasgaay-st*	*hin*	*gii*	*dang*	*k'inanning saa'ang*
and then	raised after	this	pieces	you	cut will

After it rises you cut it in pieces.

sablii	*qíhlgaay*	*stansang*	*ii uu*	*dang*	*istaa'saang*
bread	pans	4	into	you	put will

Put it into 4 bread pans.

asgaayst	*kuuskiit*	*sGwaansang*	*hawuns*	*dang*	*kaahldaa'aasaang*
and then	rise	once	once again	you	rise make will

And then let it rise once again.

'oh 45 minutes'	*dang*	*kuugaasaan*
oh 45 minutes	you	cook

Bake it about 45 minutes.

aajii	*sabliigaay*	*sga-sGwáansang*	*waast*	*dang*	*qagándaasaang*
and then	bread	one (loaf)	from	you	save

Save one loaf of dough.

taao gyaa	*Galangaa*	*dang*	*hol k'iinstaas*
oil	fry pan	you	let warm

Let some oil get hot in a fry pan.

gyaen	*sabliigaay*	*gii*	*dang*	*kinaanangsaan*	*gyaen*	*dang*	*Gaalangsaan*
and	the bread	it	you	will cut	and	you	will fry

And the bread you will cut in pieces and fry (in it).

Gaalangs   dlaas   gyaen uu aa   aa   dang   k'ii xuujuu laa'aansaan
fried   made   and   it   you   turn will
When it is brown you turn it (over in the skillet).

aajii   sabliigaay   Gaalangs   dlaas
and then   bread   fried   made
silup   suuwiit   dang   kitaansaan
syrup   sweet   you   dip
When it is fried you will dip it in sweet syrup

asgaayst   dluu   q'iihlaa   xuujuu   silupgaay   dlang   gyaes dlaas
and then   when   dish   small   the syrup   you   poured
which you have poured into a small dish.

asgaayst   waa   dlaa   Gankan   dang   niihls
and then   it   then   coffee   you   drink
And after that you drink coffee

gyaen   dang   skis   dlaa'aasaang
and   you   full   will be
and you will be full.

Raven Finds Water

yaalaay   Gantl   qíiaan   hinuu   ki'áan
raven   water   finds   this is what called
Raven Finds Water, this is what it's called.

awaahl Gagwíiuu   Gantl   Xíigalaang   tl'   súugan
a long time ago   water   dried up   they   say
A long time ago the water dried up, they say.

gam   tlíitsantl'aa   Gántl   isáangaan   tl'   súugan
not   anywhere   water   wasn't   they   say
There wasn't any anywhere, they say.

waadluu   tlíijiidaan   hlingáan   kwaayáans   hánuu
and then   anywhere   small   flowing   any
Xíigalaan   tl'   súugan
dried up   they   say
And then all the small streams dried up too, they say.

gam   tlakw   Gaa   tláahlaal   hlingei   Gan   tl'   wúnsitang
not   whatever   it   do   could   it   they   know not
**There was nothing they could do about it. They didn't know (what
to do).**

gam   tlakw   gin   Gaa   tlaahlaal   hlingei   tláa'an   isáangaan
not   whatever   thing   it   do   could   them for   wasn't
There was not any thing they could do for the people.

waadluu   yaahl   tl'aa Gáa   agan guu   gin   staláans   dluu
and then   raven   contrary   self   thing   dare   when
Gan   agán   tla   l   Gíihlgiidaayaan
it   self   made   he   ready
**And then Raven himself, on the contrary, when he was confident,
got himself ready for it.**

Gandlaayd   l   diiáang-gei-an aa
water   he   look for
He would look for the water.

waadluu   yaahl   gwáay sGáanuuwaay   deikin uu   aehl   is
and then   raven   island spirit   Hazy Island at   is
Gantl   da'áas   Gan   l   wúnsitdaan
water   owns   it   he   knew
**And then Raven knows it is the Island Spirit at Hazy Island that
owns the water.**

íkwaan   gam   nang   tl'aa   tlíijaay
but   not   one   it   where
Gandlaay is   Gan   wunsitaang aa
water   is   not   know
But no one knows where the water is.

gwaay sGaanuuwaay   sGúnaan uu   tlíijaay
island spirit   only   where
Gandlaay is   Gan   wúnsitaan
water   is   it   knows
Only the Island Spirit knows where the water is.

waadluu   yáahl   gwáayaay   aa   tluu   Gan   istáayaan
and then   raven   island   to   canoe   it   took
And then Raven took a canoe (to go) to the island.

waadluu   yáahl   tlúu   gwaa   gwáayaay   gwii   tlúu   l   qáaydaan
and then   raven   canoe   on   island   to   canoe   he   went
And then Raven started out toward the island on a canoe.

Gandlaay   l   kwahldaas   Gan uu
water   he   steal   it
aan   l   tla-Gúhlgiidaayaan   gwáay sGáanuuwaay   staa
for   he   made ready   island spirit   from
He got himself ready to steal the water from the Island Spirit.

gwáayaay   gwíi   l   tluu   qáaysaas
island   to   he   boat   went
He rowed himself toward the island.

inwáay   gwii   dluu   l   Gústluu   yáaningaay   xwujáayaanii
half   to   when   he   through   fog   blew
When he got halfway there the fog blew in.

láak   yáanuudáayaan
him   covered
The fog covered him.

uugyaen   yáaningaay   tl'atsgahl   jahlíis
and then   for   dense   too much
dluu   tlíijaan   is   l   gáawaan
when   where   is   he   lost
And then when the fog densed up too much, he's lost.

waadluu   hingáan   l   gii k'úgan-gwaan
and then   just   he   float really
And then he was just floating around there.

tlak	*gin*	*Gidáahlingaas*	*xadúu*	*uu*	*yaahl*	*gutgánggaangaan*
what	thing	do could	around		raven	think did

Raven was thinking what he could do about it.

gwáay	*sGáanuuwaay*	*laa*	*an*	*tlúu-qáatla'aas*	*dluu*
island	spirit	him	to	rowed	when

hinuu	*yáalaay*	*l*	*súudaayaan*
this	raven	he	told

When the Island Spirit arrived where the Raven was this is what he said to him:

gam	*aatlin*	*dang*	*iistlingáanangan*
not	here	you	be shouldn't

You shouldn't be here.

gam	*gín*	*tlaa*	*áatlin*	*dang*	*an*	*isanggan*	*hingáan uu*
not	thing	it	here	you	for	isn't	simply (nothing)

There's nothing here for you. Nothing.

singáay	*daGangáas*	*dang*	*ga-tlaq'iiwaasaan*	*gwaa*
weather	bad	you	it make for will	really

The weather will handicap you.

gam	*Gantl*	*gwáayaa*	*ank*	*isánggan*	*gwaa*
not	water	island	on	isn't	really

There isn't water on the island.

hínuu	*yáalaay*	*l*	*súutgaang*
this	raven	he	told

This is what he told Raven.

gam	*anqúunang-galaatang*
not	crazy be

Don't be crazy.

hin	*sanáan uu*	*gwaay sGáanuuwaay*	*laa*	*suutgaang*
this	too	island spirit	him	told

This too, Island Spirit told him.

stúhlaa	*sihlgáa*	*stúhl*	*hínuu*	*laa*	*aa*	*súutgaangaan*
turn back	back	turn back	this	him	to	said

Turn back, back, turn back. This is what he would tell him.

wáadluu	*gwáay sGáanuuwaay*	*láast*	*tlúu-qáaydaan*
and then	island spirit	him from	went

And then Island Spirit left him.

"And then when the fog densed up too much, he was lost."

yáahl   hansanáan   sihlgáang   stúhl   gans gingáan uu
raven   too   back   return   like
an   l   dlujúut
self   he   pretend
Raven, too, he pretended like he was going back.

gam   júngaa'an-gang   dáanuu   haos   gwii   l   stáelaan
not   long   while   again   to   he   turned
It wasn't long afterward he turned back again toward it.

húujii   juuyáay   qináng   an   l   xaatgáa daas
it was   sun   to   self he   way got
He used the sun to get his bearing.

gaak o-o   l   tlúu-qáagaang
it for   he   rowed
He rowed according to it.

l   tluu-qáagan   daanuu   luudaas   l   gudáangaan
he   rowed   while   surf   he   heard
While he was rowing he heard the surf.

esgaayst   l   tluu-qáagan   daanuu
after that   he   rowed   while
gwaay   gwii   luudaas   l   gudáangaan
island   on   surf   he   heard
After that while he rowed he heard the surf breaking on the island.

waadluu   táajaas   sq'út'aas   án uu   l   tluu-qáatlaagaan
and then   beach   inlet   to   he   rowed
esgaay guu   gwaay sGaanuwaay   laa   xasgadaayaan
and then   island spirit   him   welcomed
**He arrived at an inlet on the beach and the Island Spirit welcomed
him.**

chaao salii aao   laa   aan   l   qaatlaagaan
beach   him   to   he   came
He came to meet him on the beach.

yaalaay   an   l   Xángas   stist
raven   to   he   face   because
náak   hánsanaan   laak   l   dáawaan
house   too   him   he   gave
Because he was so glad to see him he invited him to his home.

uugyaen	yáal	hansanaan	l	qatúus	gingáan uu
and then	raven	too	he	thirsty	like

waa	t'álk	an	l	gíng	qatáawaan
it	more	to	he	like	thirsty

And then Raven too, as if he were thirsty, he exaggerated how thirsty he was.

gwáay	sGáanuuwaay	Gándlaay	aa	sGáalgat
island	spirit	water	it	hid

The Island Spirit (had) hidden the water.

díanuu	aa	l	sGaalgaatdaas	yaalaay	galáa'an-gwang
really	it	he	hid	raven	curious

He really made sure it was hidden. Raven was curious about it.

uugyaen	yáalaay	hansanaan	gudingáay	tláatgaas	stist
and then	raven	too	mind	strong	because

jíngaa uu uu	lei	hl	guu	l	ijáan
long	him	with	there	he	was

And then Raven too, because he had a strong mind, he was there with him for a long time.

Gándlaayk	láa	l	diáang gein
water for	his	he	looked

He was looking for his water.

tlíijaan	Gándlaay	laa	is	sGálgaasii	laa	qíeit	laa
wherever	water	his	is	hidden	his	find	his

l	gudánsdluu	laa	an	an	l	Gúudangaat
he	wished	him	to	self	he	looked suspiciously

Wishing he could find where his water was hidden, looking at him suspiciously.

Teller sings:

laa	k'yuu	Giidanggwaan	Giidanggwaan
him	for	waited	waited for

waited for him– waited for–

laa	k'yuu	l	Giidanggwaan
him	for	he	waited

He waited for him.

waast áahluu	tlak	laa	t'alk	l	xaa-hlingei	xadúu	l	gudáng
in the meantime	what	him	more	he	best could	about	he	thought

In the meantime he thought about how he could get the best of him.

Gandláayk	*l*	*stahláel gei*	*dluu*
water	he	wanted	when

When he wanted the water so badly.

hingáanuu	*tlak*	*láa*	*t'alguu*	*xálgei*	*xadúu*	*l*	*gudánggan*	*daanuu*
really	what	him	more	best	about	he	thought	while

sín Gidúu		*gwáay sGáanuwaay*	*Ga gahls*	*dluu*
suddenly by chance	island spirit	got tired	so

cha'aanuwaay	*q'wahl*	*sqwaay*	*ang*	*l*	*k'inantgan*	*daanuu*
fire	at	back	his	he	warmed	while

húu	*l*	*q'adúdéidaan*
(surprise!)	he	went to sleep (surprise!)

Really, he thought about how he could get the best of him for a long time — when suddenly, by chance, the Island Spirit got tired, so, while warming his back at the fire, he went to sleep.

waadluu	*l*	*q'adáast'áa*	*hluu*
and then	he	sleep	when

yáalaay	*kwaa*	*ú*	*st'lalingáast*		*gwii*	*l*	*ijáan*
raven	inside		rookery (where birds lay eggs)	to	he	went

hitút	*gínuwaay*	*tlii'ú*	*l*	*istáas*	*gyaen*	*uu*
bird	droppings	much	he	took	and

láa	*gwú*	*l*	*stáelaan*	*l*	*q'adáast'aahl*
him	to	he	returned	he	sleeping

gya'ándaawaay	*guut*	*laa*	*l*	*xananáangaan*
clothes	there	his	he	rubbed

And then, while he was sleeping, Raven went towards a rookery-cliff, took quite a bit of bird droppings, went back to him while he was sleeping and rubbed it all over his (Island Spirit's) clothes.

asgaayst tl'aa	*gwaay sGaanuuwaay*	*l*	*tla-skínaayaan*
after that	Island Spirit	he	woke up

And it was after that, Island Spirit woke up.

wáadluu	*láak*	*l*	*sáawaan*	*dán*	*sgwunáa*	*óyaagan*	*gwaa*
and then	him to	he	said	you	stink	much	really

And then he (Raven) said to him you stink really bad.

dán	*sgwunáa*	*óyaagan*	*gwaa*
you	stink	much	really

You stink really bad.

wáadluu   gwaay sGáanuuwaay áa   káaokw   l   diiáangaan   hluu
and then   island spirit   eggs   he   looked for   when
l   ging   sgwunáa'ang   an   l   gudáangaan
he   thing   stink   self   he   thought
**And then the Island Spirit, because he had been looking for eggs,
thought he made himself stink.**

k'aao   gyaak   l   diiáangaan   hluu
eggs   for   he   looked   because
It was because he had been looking for eggs.

k'aaok   l   diiángaan   st'áahluu   tlakw
eggs   he   looked for   meantime   what
agáng   l   tla-sgwunéi-aláan   l   gudáangaan
self   he   made   stink   he   thought
**In the meantime, while he was looking for eggs he made himself
stinky, he thought.**

waadluu   yáalaay   laa   súutgaangaan
and then   raven   him   told
agáng   hl   Gáadandaa   agáng   hl   Gáadandaa
self   (Imperative)   bathe   self   hl   bathe
And so Raven said to him; "Do bathe yourself, do bathe yourself."

waadluu   gwáay sGáanuuwaay   agáng   tlaGúhlgiidaang
and then   island spirit   self   made ready
And then Island Spirit made himself ready.

Gáadangaay   an   agáng   l   tlaGúhlgiitdaayaan
bathe   for   self   he   made ready
He got himself ready to bathe.

Gándlaay   ang   q'aaduu   ga   l   tlaGúhldaas   gyaenuu   l   qáaydaan
water   for   basket   it   he   made ready   and   he   left
He got his basket ready for the water and he left.

Gándlaay   l   dáawaan
water   he   got
He went to get water.

l   gudingáay   hlkwiidáas   t'áahl
he   mind   agitated
yáalaayk   l   kíl   gadáangaan   ga   l   k'isgadaang
raven to   he   word   bad   it   he   forgot
While he was confused, he forgot (that) he had lied to the Raven.

"He got his basket ready for the water and he left. He went to get water."

gam	Gantl	qáenggaa	ans	hinuu	laak	l	saawaan
not	water	to find	not	this	him to	he	said

That there was no water to be found is what he had said.

esgaayst uu	gwaay sGáanuwaas	náayst	xuugwíi
after that	island spirit	home	from far

gingáan uu	l	qáaydaan
like	he	walked

And after that he walked quite a ways from the house.

k'íiningaay	gwáayaayst	Xáaywaast	saa	k'yáagaas
floating moss	rock from	waves from	above	hang from

xitguu	gwaa	Gántl	xíilaas	ijáan
down	from	water	hole	was

Floating moss hanging from the rock, ground swells breaking there, hanging up above—the water hole was beneath there.

wáadluu	yáalaay	tlíijaan	Gandlaay	is	ii	l	kahl	k'íiaas
and then	raven	where	water	is	it	he	it	found

gyaen uu	laangaa	kwahldeian	gin	aangaa	l	tla-Giihlgiitdaayaan
and	his	steal	thing	his	he	made ready

And then Raven discovered where the water was and he prepared to steal his thing (the water).

gwaay	sGaanuuwaay	staa	láa	kwahldeian
island	spirit	from	he	steal

He would steal from the Island Spirit.

waadluu	sáandlaans	daals	dluu
and then	morning	early	when

naayst	agán	aan	l	kitskáaydaan
house from	his	it	he	sneaked

And then when early morning came he sneaked out from his house.

waadluu	q'áaduuwaay	áangaang	l	istáas	gyaen
and then	basket	his		he took	and

gyaak	Gántl	xíilaas	aa	l	qáaydaan
his	water	hole	to	he	walked

And then he took his water basket and he walked to where the water hole was.

waadluu	*gwa*	*l*	*Giditláas*	*gyaen uu*
and then	there	he	arrived	and

l	*katúus*	*stist*	*jíingaa uu*	*Gandlaay*	*l*	*xuhláayaan*
he	thirsty	because	long	water	he	drank

And then he arrived there and because he was thirsty he drank water for a long time.

l	*katuu*	*óyaagan*	*l*	*xuhlgyaamt*	*daayaan*
he	thirst	much	he	long drink	took

He was very thirsty. He took a long drink.

asgaayst	*laa*	*q'aaduuwaay*	*aangaa*	*l*	*st'ahdáayaan*
afterwards	his	basket	his	he	filled

Afterwards he filled up his water basket.

qut	*kunáng*	*hánsanaan*	*aangaa*	*l*	*st'ahdáayaan*
mouth	point	too	his	he	filled

He filled his beak too.

waadluu uu	*dlaa*	*gwaay*	*a k'íiwaadaas*	*iiwaans*	*gwii*	*l*	*xiidáan*
and then	after	island	situated	big	to	he	flew

And then after (he got all the water he could) he flew toward where the big island (was situated).

hawáanaan uu	*gam*	*Gantl*	*guu*	*qáenggaa 'angaan*
still (not yet)	not	water	there	see not

Still, water was not to be seen there.

waadluu	*yaahl*	*tlaagaay*	*saa*	*si'íit*	*l*	*xit-gwaansan uu*
and then	raven	land	above	high	he	flying around

Gandlaay	*qut kwunángst*	*l*	*qut gujáanggaangaan*
water	nose from	he	sprayed

And then Raven, while flying around high over the land, he sprayed the water from his nose.

Gantl	*kwaayáans*	*salii*	*gwii*	*l*	*qut gujáans*	*gyaen*
water	flowing	once	onto	he	blew	and

tlagaay	*gwii*	*l*	*qutgujáan*
land	onto	he	blew

Where water once flowed he blew (water) onto and he blew (it) onto the land.

hayaan   Gíidandaan uu   yáaningaay   qa'án   gwii   hán uu
while   condition   clouds   middle   into   even
Gándlaay   l   qut gujáanggaangaan
water   he   blew
**While he was doing this he was blowing water even into the middle
of the clouds.**

hayaan   Giidandaan uu   gwa'aa uu   iidaan
while   condition   rain   start
While this is happening it started raining.

gwa'aa uu   gaagan   daanuu   ch'íigeilaan
rain   doing   while   go on
While it is raining it doesn't stop.

wáadluu   Gándlaay   kwaayáans   iis   stahsgáan
and then   water   flowing   it   full
And then where the water used to flow it got full.

kwáhlgist   dáas   gyaen
flood   goes   and
Flood flowed and—

(speaker chants:)

Gandlaay   hans   sigáan   iijaandáan
water   too   up   was
the creeks crested—

Gandlaay   tla'aan   kwaangas   dluu   tl'   gudingáay   láagaangaan
water   them for   plenty   when   they   minds   happy
When the water got plentiful for them they were happy.

waadluu   yaahluu   hinuu   tl'   súudaayaan
and then   raven   is what they   said
yaahluu   tlagaay   qagándaayaan
raven   land   saved
And then it was Raven, they said, Raven saved the country.

aao   tlaan   gyaehlingaay   Gíidaan
it   no more   story   is
This is the end of my story.

The Octopus Story

awáahl	*xáadas*	*q'iigaans*	*dluu*
long time ago	Haidas	remember	when

gam	*núu*	*gyaehlingaay*	*wáast*	*tláangaa*	*gúu'angganaan*
not	octopus	story	from	never	lacking

A long time ago when the Haida would tell stories it was never without the story about the octopus.

hitáa	*Gandlaay*	*saagúust duu*	*yaahl*	*k'iik*
Hydaburg	Creek	north	raven	pass

láanaay	*tl'áangaa*	*xaotgáangaan*
village	theirs	lies

Their village was there at Hydaburg Creek north of North Pass.

láa gwa tláalaay sGwáansang	*t'álkuu*	*xaadaas*	*guu*	*kwaanaan*
one thousand	more	people	there	many

There were over one thousand people that lived there.

waadluu	*nuu*	*igmaay*	*qihl-tlaa-hláayaan*	*dii*	*qaa*	*saa dúutsaa*
and then	octopus	carving	flat-made	my	uncle	saa dúutsaa

And then, my uncle, Saa Duutsaa, made an octopus carving.

gyaa'ang	*Gideid*	*q'í*	*tla-ohlaangaan*
pole	about	carve	made

He made a carving about (his) totem.

yáahl qíik	*ehluu*	*laa'anga*	*gyaa'anggaangaan*	*awaahl aa*
North Pass	at	his own	pole was	years ago

His pole was at North Pass years ago.

awaahl	*xaadaas*	*gitaláng*	*gin*	*kwáan*	*sq'átitgaangaan*
back then	Haidas	children	things	many	taught did

Back then the Haida taught their children many things.

gin	*kwáan uu*	*tl'*	*Gánaatgaangaan*
things	many	they	taboo was

Many things were taboo.

gin	*kwáan*	*sanaan*	*ga*	*ángaat*	*kil*	*wáagaangaan*
things	many	too	it	fear	word	did

They put a lot of fear into their children about a lot of things.

gin	*waadluuan*	*anuu aa*	*tl'*	*kil*	*yákdánggaangaan*
things	all	for	they	word	honored

They made them respect everything.

gin   héninga   hánsan
things   living   too
gam   Gaa xudaláa   xast   náans   dlangaanggaangaan
not   children   things living   abuse not
Live things too their children should not abuse.

am   sáa   Gahl   tl'aa   tla-tisge' éitsaan
it   high   with   them   punish might
hinuu   tlaa   tl'   suutgaangaan
this   them   they   told
**"Be careful with them, child-punishment might happen" is what
they told the children.**

aaoling   tl'aa   aa   stágit   gíigaangaan
parents   them   to   from   used to do
The parents (told) them to stop many times.

gam   t'   sGatsaa'áns   aehluu   tlakw   tl'   suugaangaan
not   they mean   because   whatever   they   say
They didn't talk that way because they were mean.

gitaláng   aa   tl'   qáahliiaas   dluu
children   their they   careful   when
They were careful with their children;

tlakw   tl'aa   aa   Gatsóyaa'anggaangaan
what   them   to   careful much were
they watched over them carefully.

ahljiihluu   Gaa xudaláa   aangaan   sGatsgaangaan
that's why   children   theirs   strict
That's why they were strict with their children.

awaahl Gagwii uu
long time ago
gutilaa hanuu hlingis   yáahl   q'íik   ehl   naangaang
one right after the other North   Pass   at   lived
A long time ago they lived at North Pass one right after the other.

waagyaen   xaadas   hánsan   gutilaa án uu   gud ii   naangangaangaan
and   Haida   too   together   there   lived
And the Haidas too lived there generation after generation.

yáahl   xaatáay uu   guu   kwaan   óyaagaangaan
raven   people   there many   very were
There were many Raven people.

ch'áak'   san   guu   kwáangaangaan
eagle   too   there many were
There were a lot of Eagle clans there too.

guut   aehl   hinuut   naang   laa   áagaangaan
there at   thus   lived   they did
They lived there all together in peace.

gam   gut án   t'   skyuutgaangaangaan
not   together they quarrel didn't
They didn't quarrel with each other.

gam   gut án   tl'ehl   Gaayhltgaan   gam   anggaang
not   together they   fight   not   didn't
They never fought each other.

waadluu   q'íígangaay   aangaa   aehl   kil uu   hl   qaatlaang
and so   remembering   mine   at   word   I   come
And so my storytelling time is finally to the story.

waadluu   nang   yaahl   jáadaa   tlúu   l   istáasgyaen
and then one   raven   woman   canoe she took and
hlíın   dal   diiáng   in
away   going along   looking   rode
And then a Raven woman took a canoe and rode away (to look for roots).

l   guugan   kaóduu   gam   sihlgang   l   isáns   gyaen
she gone   a while not   back   she wasn't and
laak   tl'   diián   ins   gyaen   tluuwáay   l   qal   sGúnaanuu
her for they   look   went   and   canoe   her   empty   only
gwaay   xaat   laa   giihl   qíıgans
islands   between   hers   floating   found
laa   tl'   íıaayaan   tl'   naa'ángs   Xan hlaa aa
her (people)   they   found   their village   across
After she was gone for a while, she didn't come back and they went to look for her and her people found only her empty canoe, her boat floating between islands across from where the village is.

waadluu   tláa   aa   esgáay guu duu
and then them   for   then
nang   sGáagaas   sGunáan uu   Gán   laa   wunsit
one   Indian doctor   only   this hers   knows
And then, only an Indian Doctor for the people, he knows this about her.

núu   Gándlaay   qa'án   láanaayk   na'áangskw
octopus   water   under   village   living
gwal   l   isú   Gan   laa   l   wunsits   gyaen
there   she is   it   her   he   knows   and
sihlgáang   náa   gwii   stáelgaa   l   jigúaas
back   home   to   return   she can't
díanuu   Gan   laa   l   wunsidáan
really   it   her   he   knows

**Living in an octopus village under the water, that she is there; he
knows that about her and she is unable to return to her home, he
knew that about her for a fact.**

aa   gyaehláang   is uu   yáalaay   xaatáay   yakdáas   aehluu
it   story   is   raven   people   true   because
yáalaay   xaatáay   gudingaay   st'is   wáa   aa   xus-gudáang
raven   people   mind   sick   that   it   little better

**Because the Raven people believed this story it eased the sorrow of
the Raven people.**

hin   his   kaóduu
this   is   a while

It was like this for a while.

sáng   Gisdlúu   tl'   Gaa xudaláa   chaaosalii-k   náangaan
day   once   their children   beach on   played

One day children were playing on the beach.

nang   úhlingaa   sGwáan   nuu   gútii   táajaay
the   boy   one   octopus   baby   beach
guut   dlagándaals   l   k'áengaan
there   swimming   he   saw

One boy saw a baby octopus swimming along the ebbtide.

kwa'ú   xaat   án   l   qagánt   sánsdliiya
rocks   on   self   he   save   tried

He was trying to save himself among the rocks.

waadaal   íkw   Gáalges   dluu
then   to   dark   when
nuu   gútiigaay   an   tla-xíninggéihls   gyaen
octopus   baby   self   made changed   and
náa'anlang   aa   l   st'aa'ójaawaagaan
grandparents   to   he   visited

**The day before, when it became dark, the baby octopus changed
himself to human form and went to visit his grandparents.**

gam	*laa*	*tl'*	*skitáns*	*dluu*
not	him	they	recognize	when

gé	*léi*	*ii*	*tl'*	*ánjuuaangaan*
no	him	to	they	pay attention didn't

They didn't recognize him, they didn't even pay attention to him.

Gaagáay	*t'iits*	*chaaosalii-k*	*naangs*	*sqáangw*	*jándaa*	*daa'áayaan*
children	some	beach on	playing	sticks	long	had

Some children playing on the beach had some long sticks.

Gahl	*gin*	*l*	*kitgúnuugaangaan*
with (them)	things	they	poked

With them they poked things.

nuu	*gíitii*	*is*	*l*	*qíngwaas*	*Gahl*	*l*	*náangitaawaan*
octopus	baby	is	they	see	with it	they	play did

Seeing the baby octopus they started playing with it.

l	*aaoláng*	*laa*	*aa*	*stigíidaangaan*	*ga*	*l*	*q'íisgataawaan*
their	parents	them	to	warned		it	they	forgot

They forgot their parents' instructions warning them not to do things.

gin	*Gánaas*	*laak*	*tl'*	*súutuugaangaan*
thing	taboo	them to	they	told

hansan	*ga*	*l*	*q'iisgitaawaan*
too	it	they	forgot

They forgot, too, the instructions about things taboo they told them.

nuu	*gútiigaay*	*chaaosalíí*	*gwii*	*l*	*k'ikáat*	*sánshluugaangaan*
octopus	baby	beach	onto	they	flip	tried

They tried to flip the baby octopus onto the beach.

nuu	*gútiigaay*	*Gándlaay*	*gwii*
octopus	baby	water	into

an	*l*	*qagánt*	*sanstlgaangaan*
self	he	save	tried

The octopus baby tried to save himself into the water.

an	*l*	*qagándaas*	*gyaen*
self	he	saved	and

sihlgáang	*nuu*	*tlagaay*	*gwii*	*l*	*stáelaan*
back	octopus	land	into	he	returned

He saved himself and went back to the octopus village.

gam	gin	an	tl'	wúnsitaangaan uu
not	thing	self	they	know not

a	nuu	gútii	is	yáahl	jáadaas	gít uu	ijáan
it	octopus	baby	is	raven	woman's	child	is

What they didn't know was the octopus baby was the child of Raven Woman.

nuu	gútiigaay	sihlgáang	nuu	laangaay	gwii	stáelaan	dluu
octopus	baby	back	octopus	village	to	returned	when

nuu	xaatgáay	gudingáay	hlkwiid	istláayaan
octopus	people	minds	moving	became

When the octopus baby got back to the octopus village the octopus people got excited.

tlakw	nuu	gútiigaay	aa	tl	tlaahlaalaan	tlaa	an	st'igáan
what	octopus	baby	to	they	did	them	to	angered

What they (the children) had done to the octopus baby made them angry.

nuu	xaatgáay uu	sGáw uu	gináang	ansaáayaan
octopus	people	payment	property	ask

tlakw	nang	xaaxuujúus	tláa	tl'	istáayaan
what	the	child	theirs	they	did

The octopus people were going to ask for payment for what they did to their child.

xánggaang	xáadas	tl'	isdáa'ansaáas	Gan	an	tl'	xúhlgiidaayaan
revenge	people	they	do would	it	self	they	decided

They made up their minds to take revenge on the people.

waast ahluu	nang	sGáagaas	tlakw	gin	Gits	qáengaan
meanwhile	the	indian doctor	what	things	going on	saw

The Indian Doctor had a vision of what was going on.

tlakw	gin	Gaa xudalgáay	isdáayaan	Gaatgáaykw	l	suudaayaan
what	thing	children	did	people to	he	told

He told the people what the children had done.

tlakw	Gaa xudalgáay	gin	tla-Gidáanuu	Gaatgáayk	l	súudaayaan
what	children	thing	made result	people to	he	told

He told the people the result of what the children had done.

uugyaen	*gin*	*sGwáansang*	*san*	*nang*	*yaahl*	*jáadaas*
and then	thing	one	too	the	raven	woman

xaatgáay	*l*	*qíntdang*	*sinslaas a*	*sanáan uu*	*l*	*qáangáan*
people	she	warn	tried	too	he	saw

And then one thing too the Raven Woman tried to warn the people, he saw.

tlakw	*gin*	*Gíidansaáas*	*láanaay-k*	*l*	*súudaayaan*
what	thing	be would	village to	he	told

He told the village how it was going to be.

nuu	*xaatáay uu*	*tl'aa*	*an*	*yaalaay*	*xaatáay*	*an*
octopus	people	them	to	raven	people	to

Gaayhlt	*intláa'an ansaáas*	*tl'áa-k*	*l*	*suudaayaan*
fight	come would	them to	he	told

The octopus people were coming to fight the raven people, he told them.

xúuts	*naay*	*xadúu*	*an*	*tl'*	*Gíihldaa ansaáas*
bear	house	around	self	they	spread would

yáalaay	*xaatáay*	*tlangánja'áa*	*an*	*tl'*	*Giihlgiidaay*
raven	people	ready	self	they	prepare

They would spread themselves around Brown Bear House, the Raven people (should) get themselves ready.

Gaagáay	*tlakw*	*gin*	*tla-gúusuuweialaan uu*
children	what	thing	did

tlii	*tl'áa*	*an*	*st'igáan*
much	them	to	angry

The trouble the children had made made them angry at them.

ch'áak'	*xaatáay*	*sanaan*	*gwa*	*na'áanaan*	*kyáanaan uu*
eagle	people	too	there	lived	but

gam	*asgáay*	*ii*	*tl'*	*gudáa'angaan*
not	that	to	they	mind didn't

The Eagle people lived there too but they didn't pay attention to them.

"The octopus people came from the water onto the beach, towards the chief's house, and crawled up on top."

D. PASCO

nang   íitl'aakdáas   xaatgáayk   aangaa   sáawaan
the   chief   people to   his   said
Gáayhldaa   an   hl   an   Gíihlgiit uu
fight   for   (Imperative)   self ready
waahlahl   tl'   ginángs,   nuu   xaatáay   ginángs
potlatch   they   demand   octopus   people   demand
gam   hlingáan   Gii   tlang   gudáa ansaan
not   can   it   we   pay attention will
**The chief told his own people to make themselves ready to fight;
they're demanding payment, the octopus people are demanding, we
can't pay attention to what they want.**

nang sGáagaas   tlak   gin   Gíit ansa aas   tláak   l   súudaas
indian doctor   what   thing would be ~~   them to he   told
gyaen   Gan   an   Giihlgiideit   hánsanaan   tl'aa-k   l   suudaayaan
and   it   self ready   too   them to   he   told
**The Indian Doctor told them the way things would be and he told
them to get themselves ready for it too.**

náay   áangaa   hl   tla-skúuhlduu
home   your   (Imperative)   make secure
Make your house secure!

ginatgaay   san   aangaa   tl-skúuhlduu
smoke hole   too   your   seal
Seal the smoke hole too!

sángyaas   dluu   tl'   Gaayhlt   íntlaa'aa'ánsa'aan
night   when   they   fight   come will
When night comes they come to fight.

tl'   sáayaan   gingáan uu   gin   Gidáan
they   said   like   thing was
It was exactly like they said.

nuu   xaatáay   Gándlaay-st   chaaoosalíi   gwii
octopus   people   water from   beach   onto
nang   íitl'aakdáas   gyaa   naay   gwii
the   chief   his   house   to
isgyaen   únguut   áan   tluu   istáalgaalaang
and   onto   on   crawl   went
**The octopus people, from the water onto the beach, crawled towards
the chief's house and crawled up on top.**

nang	ùtl'aakdáas	isgyaen	xaatgáay	tl'	tla- Gaqùtuugaasaang
the	chief	and	people	they	make drown would

They would suffocate the chief and the people.

hin uu	tl'	gudaangaan	nuu	xaatáay aa
this	they thought		octopus	people

This is what they thought, the octopus people.

sangáay	istluu	nuu	xaatáay	Ga	áng	jigù'istláayaan
morning	it is	octopus	people	it	not	couldn't do

Towards morning (it became clear that) the octopus people couldn't do it.

tl'	gudáangaan	iiláa tlaa
they	planned	but

sihlgáang	Gándlaay	gwii	tl'	st'ùhliidaan
back	water	to	they	returned

Instead of what they had planned they started back to the water.

cha'ansùst	ámjuuwaan	isgéi aa	nuu	xaatáay	jigù'aayaan
water from	long	be	octopus	people	couldn't

The octopus people couldn't be out of the water for a long time.

nuu	xaatáay	tlakw	ga	kìhl hlaayaan	waa aa	jigù'aas	gyaen
octopus	people	what	it	attack	it	couldn't	and

nang	ùtl'aakdáas	gyaa	naay	san	tl'	qagándaayaan
the	chief	his	house	too	they	saved

The attack of the octopus people failed and they saved the chief's house too.

dat	gwajaaw	gei'anuu	nang	ùtl'aakdáas	wáahlahl	ùwaanaan
it	celebration	be	the	chief	potlatch	big

To commemorate, the chief gave a big potlatch.

waadluu	tl'	gutilaa	dáas	gyaen	nang	yáahl	jáadaas	isgyaen
and then	they	together	gave	and	the	raven	woman	and

nuu	gitù	hansan	Gan	t'	yakwdáa'an
octopus	baby	too	it	they	honored

And then they made up and they honored Raven Woman and the octopus baby too.

hítgyaa	xaatgáay	gyaehlingaay uu	aa	ùjing
this	Haida	story	it	is

This is a Haida story.

dii   q'aa   saa dúuts   Gahl   gyaahlántgiinii
my   uncle   Saa Duuts   it   tell used to
uugyaen   san   gin   l   q'it'giinii   gyáa 'an   a   gyaahláan   ist
and   too   things   he   carve used to   pole   it   story   is
**My uncle Saa Duuts used to tell about it and also the things he used
to carve is what this story is about.**

l   q'itdáanuu   jingaa uu   hl   da'áang
his   carving   long ago   I   heard
I heard about his carving long ago.

aao   tlaan   gyaehlingaay   Gíidang
it   no more   story   is
That's all of my story.

The Story of **qaao qaao**, or Quoth the Raven, "Nevermore"

awáahl Gagwíi   gáada   eihl   gin   iijáan uu
a long time ago Carta Bay at   thing was
A long time ago something happened at Carta Bay.

Gaa hl   dláng-k   hl   gyaehlándaa'ansa'aan
it with   you for   I   story make will
I will story-make for you with it.

yáahl   Gidéid uu   aa   újing
raven   about it   it   is
It's about a raven.

chíin   tl'   xiláandaas   dluu   xaatgáay   xaa-ch'aagáangaan-giinii
fish   they   dry make   when   people   all move there used to
When they dried fish the people used to all move there.

esgáay guu   chíinaay   tl'   xilágíigaangaan
and there   fish   they   dry always
And they always dried the fish there.

cháanuut   geihls   k'iáahl   guu   Gaa   tl'   ch'aak   xuujúugaangaan
fall   become   every time there   to   they   move   all do
Every fall they moved there as a group.

sáng   Gid uu   hayáan   chíinaay   aa   hlGáng uu   l   gaandaan
day   certain   while   fish   on   still   they   worked
On a certain day they were working on the fish.

aa   tl'   k'yáatiid-eihl uu   yáalaay   yáahl   is
there they   hang start become   raven   raven   is
chíinaay   tl'áangaa   l   q'uhldiidaan
fish   theirs   he   steal start
When they started hanging (their fish) there, Raven, a particular raven, started stealing their fish.

yáahl   guu   kwáangúigaangaan
ravens   there many always
There were always many ravens there.

uugyaen   aayáahl   is uu   l   "tricky"gaagaangaan
and   raven   is   he   tricky was
And this raven, he was tricky.

l   kudingáagaangaan
he   clever state was
He was clever.

tl'aa   t'alk   l   Gil-gii-gaangaan
them   more   he   beat always did
He always got the best of them.

chínaay   tl'áa   l   q'uhldáasii,   unguut   tl'áa   l   qáawansii
fish   their   he   steal   on top   their   he   walk
tl'áa   l   xa-dáaGangiit,   Gii   tl'áa   l   xa-jahlnanáng
their   he   claw-ruin   into   their   he   claw-shred
He, stealing their fish, walking on top of them, he claw-ruins them,
he claw-shreds into them.

wáadluu   sang   Gidáas   nang   úhlingaa   sáawaan
then   day   certain   a   man   said
And so on a certain day a man said:

huu   yáahl   is uu   hl   tiiyáa'ansa'aan
this   raven   is   I   kill will
I'm gonna kill that raven.

waadluu   hlGiitgaay   aal   l   isdáas   gyaen
and then   bow   his   he   took   and
hlkyáansgangaay   qáahlii   aa   an   l   sgáalaan
bushes   inside   in   self   he   hid
And then he took his bow and arrow and hid himself in the bushes.

hayáan   l   Gídaadaan   hayáan   guu   l   q'aógandaan
while   he   state was   while   there   he   sit
yáalaay   xiitlaa'áayaan
raven   flew to
While he was in there, while he was sitting there, the raven flew in.

guu   áan   l   sgáalgaadaas   gam   yáalaay   qíngangaan
there   in   him   hiding   not   raven   see not
The raven didn't see him hiding there.

waadluu   laa   l   xagwasáan   kaóduu   láa   l   ch'agáan
then   him   he   aimed at   while   him   he   shot
Then he aimed at him for a while . . . he shot him.
wáadluu   gwaa   salíiaa uu   gam   waast   jíngaa'anggaan
and then   true   after there   not   from   long time not
daanuu   yáalaay   tl'   wáadluaan uu   xitlaayiidáan
when   ravens   they all   fly to start
And then not long afterwards the ravens all started flying in.

wáakw   tl'   taq'aagudáas-gwaan
there   their   talk really
Their talk was really something.

tl'áa	an	st'igáanang	nang	sGwáansang	tl'		ch'agáan
them	self	angry	a	one		someone	shot

It made them mad (that) someone shot one of them.

tlakw	yáalaay	súus	gam	xaatgáay	Gan	wúnsitang
whatever	ravens	say	not	people	that	understand not

The people don't understand what the ravens are saying.

íkwaan	nang	sGwáansang uu	yaahl	kíl	an	l	únsidaang
but	a	one	raven	language	self	he	understands

But there was one person, he understands raven language.

Gán	k'aldingáagaanii	tlíi	yáahl	kíl	an	únsitsii
that	amazing	much	raven	language	self	understands

It was really an amazing thing, the understanding of raven language.

ahljíıhluu	tlakw	gin	iijáangaan	Gán	l	únsitaan
therefore	whatever	thing	was	that	he	understands

So whatever happened, he understood.

tlakw	yáalaays	suus	Gan	l	únsit
whatever	ravens	say	that	he	understands

Whatever the ravens say he understands.

wáastáahluu	waa	t'álk uu	yáalaay	wáak	an	k'áasgit
meanwhile	there	more	ravens	there	self	increase

Meanwhile there were getting to be more and more ravens there.

yíngaan	waak	skúulaas	gyaen uu	Gándlaay	in- gúust uu	iijing
simply	there	crowded	and	water	across	is

It was really crowded there across the creek.

kwáan	eihl	jahlíısii uu	tl'áa	an	sángiitsaa-géilaan
many	because	mixed up	they	self	disturbed become

Because many of them mixed together they become disturbed.

nang	sGwáansang	yáahl	kíl		an	únsitaanuu	tlakw
a	one	raven	language		self	know	whatever
gin	is	Gan	l	unsits	tl'áan	aa	l	gyúulaanggaangaan
thing	is	that	he	knew	them	to	he	listened

As for the one-who-understood-raven-language, he listened to them and he understood whatever was going on.

húugwaa	nang	an	tla-yakdáns	húugwaa	gin	haganáan
truly	one	self	make honor	truly	reason	ravens
yáalaay	wáadluaan	qáahlii	gans gingáan	xuujúus
all		angry	like	all

That he was a truly honorable one is truly the reason why all the ravens were acting like they were angry.

"And then he took his bow and arrow and hid himself in the bushes."

yáahl   kíl   an   nang   únsits uu
raven   language   self   one   knows
tlakw   súus   Gan   l   únsitaan
whatever   say   that   he   knows

**The one-who-understands-raven-language, he understood whatever
was said.**

yáalaay   an   st'igán   gwaa   nang   istlúujuu   git   gwaa   iijáan
ravens   self   angry   true   one   dignified   child   true   was

**It is the case that the ravens are truly angry, it was truly the child
of a dignified one.**

húugwaa   nang   útl'aakdáas   git   gwaa   iijáan
truly   one   chief   child   true   was

Truly it is the case it is a rich man's child.

yáalaay   tl'áa   an   st'ihl   nang   yáahl   kíl   an
ravens   they   self   angry-become   one   raven   language   self
l   unsits   láa uu   Gan   únsitgaangaan
he   knows   he   that   understood
nang   útl'aakdáas   git   úhlingaa   isú
one   chief   child   boy   is

**The one-who-understands-raven-language, he is the one who did
understand that the ravens were getting themselves angry especially
because the chief's child is a boy.**

yáalaay   Gaayhlt-iits   wáak   an   q'ásgits
ravens   fight-begin   there   self   increase
waak   an   q'asgits   waa   t'alk   úsdluu
there   self   increase   there   more   when

The bickering of the ravens increased and increased.

chínaay   tl'áa'aangga   tla-kwaanaan uu   tliijiidaan uu   xakw-jáangaan
fish   their own   any way   any where   claw-threw

**They were claw-throwing their (the people's) fish any way, any
where.**

wáadluu   xaatgáay   gwatsihldáayaan
and so   people   worry begin

And so the people began to worry.

nang yáahl kil an únsits láa uu
one raven language self know he
tl'áa-k súudaayaan gin haganaan tlii yáalaay kwáansii
them to say reason much ravens many

The understander-of-raven-language is who told them the reason (for) so many ravens (being there).

húugwaa wáadluu tl'áa-k l sáawaan
truly and then them to he said
nang utl'aakdáas git uu aa íijing gwaa nang tl' ch'agánaa
one chief's child it is true one they shot

And then truly he told them this: it is the case that the one (raven) they shot is the chief's child.

l ki'íuu qaao qaao
his name qaao qaao

His name is *qaao qaao*.

wáadluu húugwaa yáalaay qaao qaao
and then truly ravens qaao qaao
hin súugans gingáan uu tl' kyáagaanggaangan
this said like they called
qaao qaao tl' tiiyáang, qaao qaao tl' tiiyáang
qaao qaao they killed, qaao qaao they killed

And then indeed, the ravens sounded as if qaao qaao is what they said (as) they cried "they killed *qaao qaao*, they killed *qaao qaao*."

nang yáahl tl' tiiyáayaan
the raven they killed
hluu tlakw yáalaay kyáadaan xajúu
is what whatever ravens called all

The raven they killed is what the ravens were all calling (about).

wáadluu xaatgaay hínuu gwáalaan tlakw Gan uu
and then people this thought whatever that
tl'áak an sgáaosaan nang utl'aakdáas git tl'ang tiiyáayaan
them to self pay will the chief's child we killed

And then the people thought this: we will pay for it that we killed the chief's child.

sihl tl' gwadáangaan tlakw láa-k isdáasii
back they thought whatever him to did
wáadluu gútiláa Gidéiduu tl' gúusuu-iidaan
and then make up about they talk start

They regretted what happened to him and so they started to talk about making up.

yáalaay   an   tl'áng   gútiláa   dáasaan   hinuu   tl'   súus uu
ravens   to   we   make up   do will   this   they   say
"We will make up to the ravens," this is what they said.

wáadluu   chínaay   wáadluaan uu   chínaay   kwáan   xustliiéi uu
and then   fish   all   fish   many   possible
yáalaay   an   tl'   k'yáadaayaan
ravens   for   they   hang
And then, all the fish, as many fish as possible, they hung up for the ravens.

tl'   tla-xíı-guhl   gudáng
they   make dry start   try
wáadluu   nang   iitl'aakdáas   an   tl'   Gayáayaan
and then   the   chief   to   they   invited
They began to try to dry (fish) and then they invited the chief.

nang   yáahl   kíl   an   l   únsitan uu
the   raven   language   self   he   knows
xaatgáayk   sáawaan   nang   útl'aakdáas   xitlas'áa'ansaan
people to   said   the   chief   fly to here will
The one-who-understands-raven-language told the people "The chief will fly here."

uugyaen   hawáns   laa   kyuu   tl'   Gńt
and then   again   him   waiting for   they   are
And then they wait for him.

láa   kyuu   tl'   Gńt   kaóduu
him   wait for   they   are   a while
They wait for him a while. . . .

laa   an   tl'áa   Gńt   tl'   suut   nang   útl'aakdáas uu   xitla'áa'ansa'aan
him   for   they   wait   they   say   the   chief   fly to here will
They say to wait for him, the chief will fly here.

l   duungéihl   tláas   dluu   láa   tl'   qingáadaang
he   close become   them   when   them   they   pass the word (make see)
When he comes close they pass the word to them.

waa   gingáan uu   nang   útl'aakdáas   xitlaa'áa'aan
this   like   the   chief   flew to
Just like this (as they said), the chief arrived.

yáahl   íıwaan   xustliiéi uu   iijáan
raven   big   possible   was
The raven was the biggest possible.

Gan k'aldingáasii Gan k'aldingáagang tlíi l íiwaans
what amazing what amazing much he big
uugyaen yáahl hlGáhlgans iiláa uu l xúhlahl Xángan
and ravens black but he blue looks

It was amazing, it was amazing how big he was, and while ravens are black (usually), he looked blue.

qíidaay ank uu l q'áwaas dluu
tree on he sat when
l xúhlahl Xángansii Gán tl' k'aldingáa
he blue looked that they amazed

When he sat there on the tree he looked so blue that it amazed them.

wáast áahluu yáalaay guu ijáan
meanwhile ravens there were
Gándlaay ingúust sGeihlgaangaan
water across cried out

Meanwhile the ravens that were across the creek cried out.

tl' kyáagaans an sGéihl
they call self cry
aao nang útl'aakdáas íijing, aao nang útl'aakdáas íijing
here the chief is here the chief is

They call, crying to themselves, "Here is the chief, here is the chief!"

tl' suugan kaoduu
they said while

They said it a while. . . .

nang yáahl íiwaans gudingáang l tláats-geihldaas gyaen uu
the raven big mind he strong made and
chínaay aa l xitáa-ihl wáadluu gyaehlingaay hinuu Gúdang
fish to he fly start and then story this is

The big raven makes his mind strong and starts to fly to the fish and then the story is this:

chínaay aa l xitéihls dluu l hldanúugan daanuu l
fish to he fly start when he feast started when he
táatlingaas t'álk uu l hldanáawaan an l stádaangaan
eat could more he feast self he filled up

When he flew down to the fish, as he continued to eat he ate more than he could hold; he filled himself up.

l   sk'ísdlaas   dluu   tláan   l   wáadaan
he filled   when   no more he   did
When he was filled to bursting, he quit.

nang   útl'aakdáas   hldanúugan   kaóduu   hínuu   l   sáawaan
the   chief   feasted   a while   this   he   said
The chief feasted a while and then said this:

dú   git   dláng   tiiyáayaan
my   child you   killed
"You killed my child."

nang   tiiyáayaan uu   da   an   hl   ging   qúsgútsaan
the   killed   it   self I   try   forget will
"I will try to forget the killed one."

yaats   xaataay   "forgive"   hínuu   suugan
white   people   forgive   this way say
White people say it this way, "forgive."

l   gín   l   tla-sgudáayaan   gwaa   dú   gitaa
his thing he   make mistake   true   my   child
ahljúhluu   láa   gatiiyáayaan
therefore   him   killed
"He really made a mistake in this deed, my child did, therefore he got killed."

láagan,   láagan
good   good
"It's okay now, it's okay."

áajiidlaa   tláan   hagwán   xaagáay   aa   hl   kil   wáa'asaan
after this   never   same   people   to   I   word   do will
wáadluu   tl'   galaadáa
and then   they   good do
"I'll tell the (raven) people never (to do) this same thing after this and they will be good."

salii aa uu   l   xitláast
afterward   he   flew from
Afterwards he flew away.

xíts   gyaen   salíuu   yáalaay   ingúust   láa   kyuu   Gidáan
fly   and   after   ravens   across   him   waiting for are
hahlgwú   chínaay   gwú   xit   xujúus   gyaen uu   tl'   hldanúu
to here   fish   towards fly   all   and   they   feasted
And after flying away, the ravens waiting for him across the creek all flew over here to the fish and they feasted.

tl'   wáadluaan   an   sk'ishlúudaas
they   all   self full make
esgaayst uu   sta   tl'   xit   xujuu'áawaan
and then   from   they   fly   all
They all made themselves full and then they all flew away.

wáadlaa uu   tláan   yáahl   isgyaen
after that   no more   ravens   and
xaatgáay   gwaa   an   Gaayhltga'ángaan
people   true   self fight not
After that there were no more ravens and the people didn't fight among themselves.

yakiiáagan   dláng   gyaehlándaa   hl   súudaas
true   you   story   I   tell
The story I told you was true.

gáadaa   eihl uu   ijáan   yakiiáagan   a   gyaehlángwaas
Carta Bay   at   was   true   it story
It truly happened at Carta Bay, the story.

References

Blackman, Margaret. 1973. "The Northern and Kaigani Haida: A Study in Photographic Ethnohistory." Unpublished Ph.D. dissertation, Ohio State University.

Cogo, Robert. 1979. *Haida Story Telling Time.* Susan Horton, ed. Ketchikan Indian Corporation.

Dawson, George. 1881. *On the Haida Indians of the Queen Charlotte Islands.* Geological Survey of Canada, Report of Progress for the Years 1878-79.

Day, A. G. 1951. *The Sky Clears. Poetry of the American Indian.* Macmillan.

Eastman, Carol M. 1985. "Establishing Social Identity through Language Use." *Journal of Language and Social Psychology* 4(1): 1-20.

Eastman, Carol M., and Paul K. Aoki. 1978. "Phonetic Segments of Haida (Hydaburg Dialect)." In Mohammed Ali Jazayery, Edgar C. Polomé, and Werner Winter, eds., *Literary Studies in Honor of Archibald A. Hill. Vol. II, Descriptive Linguistics.* Mouton.

Eastman, Carol M., and Elizabeth A. Edwards. 1984. *Contextualizing Cues in Haida Narrative.* Paper presented at 19th International Conference on Salishan and Other Languages. August. University of Victoria, Victoria, B.C., Canada.

Edwards, Elizabeth A. 1979. "Topic Marking in Haida." *International Journal of American Linguistics* 45(2): 49-57.

——————— 1982. "The Importance of Pragmatic Factors in Haida Syntax." Unpublished Ph.D. dissertation, University of Washington.

——————— 1983. "Focus and Constituent Order in Haida." *Canadian Journal of Linguistics* 28(2): 149-57.

Enrico, John. 1980. *Masset Haida Phonology.* Ann Arbor: University Microfilms International.

Forgas, Joseph A. 1979. *Social Episodes: The Study of Interaction Routines.* Academic Press.

Gumperz, J., ed. 1982. *Language and Social Identity. Studies in Interactional Sociolinguistics, Vol. II.* Cambridge University Press.

Halliday, M. A. K. 1967. *Notes on Transitivity and Theme in English, Part II.* Journal of Linguistics 3: 199-244.

Hodge, Frederick W. 1905. *Handbook of American Indians North of Mexico.* Smithsonian Institution, Bureau of American Ethnology.

Hymes, Dell, H. 1981. "In Vain I Tried to Tell You." *Essays in Native American Ethnopoetics.* Philadelphia: University of Pennsylvania Press.

Krause, Aurel. 1956 (1885). *The Tlingit Indians*. Translated by Erna Gunther. University of Washington Press.

Leer, Jeff. 1977. *Introduction. Haida Dictionary*. Society for the Preservation of Haida Language and Literature. Fairbanks, Alaska.

Murdoch, George Peter. 1934a. "Kinship and Social Behavior Among the Haida." *American Anthropologist* 36: 355-85.

——————— 1934b. "The Haidas of British Columbia." In *Our Primitive Contemporaries*. Macmillan, New York.

Powell, John W. 1880. *Introduction to the Study of Indian Languages*. 2nd ed. Washington, D.C.

Reid, Bill, and Robert Bringhurst. 1984. *The Raven Steals the Light*. University of Washington Press.

Swanton, John R. 1905. *Contributions to the Ethnology of the Haida*. New York: G. E. Strechert.

——————— 1911. *Haida Grammar. Handbook of American Indian Languages*. *BAE Bul* 40(2): 205-81.

Thompson, Nile. 1985. "Twana Baby Talk Theoretical Implications." Unpublished Ph.D. dissertation, University of Washington.

Vaughan, J. Daniel. 1984. "Toward a New and Better Life: Two Hundred Years of Alaskan Haida Culture Change." Ph.D. dissertation, University of Washington.

Young, Samuel Hall. 1927. *Hall Young of Alaska, "The Mushing Parson."* New York and Chicago, Fleming H. Revell Co.